CONNELL BERNARD

NOW THE DAY IS OVER

VIKING

VIKING

Penguin Books Ltd, Harmondsworth, Middlesex, England
Viking Penguin Inc., 40 West 23rd Street, New York, New York 10010, U.S.A.
Penguin Books Australia Ltd, Ringwood, Victoria, Australia
Penguin Books Canada Ltd, 2801 John Street, Markham, Ontario, Canada L3R 1B4
Penguin Books (N.Z.) Ltd, 182–190 Wairau Road, Auckland 10, New Zealand

First published 1985

Typeset in VIP Palatino

Typeset, printed and bound in Great Britain by
Hazell Watson & Viney Limited,
Member of the BPCC Group,
Aylesbury, Bucks

British Library Cataloguing in Publication Data
Bernard, Connell
    Now the day is over.
    I. Title
    823'.914[F]   PR6052.E63[

ISBN 0-670-80828-8

'Now the day is over
Night is drawing nigh,
Shadows of the evening
Steal across the sky . .'

S. Baring-Gould,
Hymns Ancient and Modern

TO MY WIFE, DANY, AND MY DAUGHTERS
BETHENEY AND CARRIE; WITH LOVE.

That the day does come – and go – for all of us, is not to be denied; yet we never seem to think so at the time, that it can ever quite be over. This is how it was, and still is, some of it. Only I have changed. I know that now it is too late. Mesmerising Time, that old illusionist, had but to stand aside and watch me going by. And there I was, gone!

Where once I was there can be no returning. And that's life's little tragedy. We always lose our way.

★1★

★

It was one of those still, stifling-hot afternoons in mid-June, not a breath of air, not a whisper anywhere; bright as a burnished bugle, the sun lay directly overhead, blaring down out of a sky bleached the colour of dying cornflowers with all the pitiless application of a painter's blowlamp. Shade, there was none, and no respite from the worst of the glare. Glistening tar gone liquid as black treacle bubbled up from winding lanes set in a sweltering green riot of summer hedgerows, and birds on the verges, throats gaping like snapdragons, drooped with dry fanned-out wings among the parched grass and wilting roadside flowers.

Save for a grasshopper population which sawed and arrowed, swift as crossbow darts, above the arid dust that passed for soil, nothing, no thing, stirred. It was a pause, at deadlock, yet only a lull in the age-old struggle for supremacy between earth and elements, no quarter asked nor given.

The very silence was exhausting.

The location, the borders of England and Wales; that no-man's-land, the strip of middle, parting one place from the other. Neither daft and comical Welsh Wales where vowels were rich and throaty, nor yet the placid classic shires of England, where they spoke the thin language so despised by some. Just land left lying somewhere, impartially blending the characters of two.

Hung in balance between planes of national identity a mirage was shimmering, remote as far Tibet, as beckoning as Samarkand, mysterious as both.

And hot as a baker's oven.

Making no concessions to the weather except for a moist lettuce leaf placed thoughtfully on the thinning brilliantined hair under his brown bowler hat, a big fat man, bland of countenance, middle-aged and pink of flesh, sat waiting on the stone capping of the humpback bridge that looked down on the station at Clanetty. Clanetty was beyond the back of beyond, stuck in the middle of nowhere some way from its namesake village, the last but one halt on the pretty little branch-line which meandered off the beaten track from here to there and back again.

In spring the tangled banks of the railway cutting were a mass of primroses and cowslips, followed on among the ferns and catkins by bluebells, violets and pale wild daffodils, and two or three times a week a one-coach train trundled by so gently and at peace with all the world it barely disturbed the choral rise of skylarks. Nesting whitethroats and robins ignored it, and families of rabbits on the bank could hardly be bothered to hop away from so benign an intruder.

Perhaps even, in this beautiful hidden place, lost now in the profusions of the summer, they did not think of the train as intruder at all. It came by, was momentarily there, and just as suddenly, in a wisp and a wavery whistle, like an apparition it was gone.

The fat man – my Uncle Wallace – had on a light flannel shirt, close-striped, like the ticking on a bolster, a loose snuff-coloured cardigan knitted by Aunt Jessie, bookie's trousers in a big check pattern, cut generous round the seat, and brown boots whose toecaps shone in the brass-bright afternoon like new conkers.

His open cheery face was smoothshaven and deceptively innocent, with the minimum of features, like a child's drawing of the sun.

What a mistake it was to write him off as anybody's fool.

It's one of my biggest assets in life, he would say, being taken for a gawby.

Sucking a ha'penny gobstopper to moisten his mouth, he had presently strayed along a byway of memory, wholly now absorbed in looking at himself, a strapping young man long years ago getting off the same smart maroon-painted train – the *Princess Alice* – that was bringing me

11

to meet him, and was deeply unaware of the furnace heat of the summer's day.

★　★

The little knot of war-weary soldiers quit the compartments, tiredly slinging down a heap of packs and kitbags before they stepped onto the platform, dispirited young men grown old in battle and trembling with relief at being home.

Some were eaten up with trench fever, others stunned with shellshock or the death, in droves, of friends; else doomed to cough their nights out, like Uncle Fred and Uncle Bert, from the sickening effects of mustard gas.

None of them seemed really in possession of himself. True, they were there; but in a sense not where they were. Denatured by experiences, they were at most the remnants of their former selves.

Only their eyes, persisting sparks of hope in husks of resignation, showed they were anywhere alive at all.

Demobilisation procedure at some reception centres had fallen into only a token as the troops poured back from France after the Great War and these eleven men, all uncles of mine bar two, had been ferried back to an English port, packed like kippers in a crate, counting themselves fortunate to be issued a communal travelling warrant to take them up to London, and thence home.

Nobody seemed to care. They spent two days and nights on soup and bread handed out by voluntary organisations, sleeping rough on platform benches, before a harassed captain from Military Transport sent them off to Birmingham, thankfully out of his area, taking their names, ranks and numbers and informing them they would be advised by the War Office where later to hand in kit and uniforms.

Shunted round from pillar to post they reached

Shrewsbury eventually, transferring then to the connecting local puffers which had brought them thus far.

'Buck up, my lucky lads,' rallied Uncle Dick. 'It's beginning to smell like home.'

'Home for the Ready Boys of the Wrekin.' Uncle Wallace sniffed the air appreciatively. 'Sometimes I thought we'd never see it again.'

'Some won't,' said Uncle Mogg the sniper.

Drawn to the point of emaciation, his steely eyes betrayed his state of mind, and haggard cheeks an illness closing in.

'Our Jim and Ellis for a start.'

He named the two uncles I was never to know, left wrapped in shrouds of guncloth beside a Flanders ditch.

'I hadn't forgotten,' said Uncle Wallace quietly. 'Nor Joe Watkins . .'

'. . and Happy Price and Emlyn Brandreth . .' put in softspoken Uncle Bert. 'I used to like Happy. He always made me laugh. They say he died of wounds.'

'. . and Ifor and Eric Plimmer,' continued Uncle Teddie. 'We'll have to call and pay respects.'

'. . and little Sammy Ball and Noah Parry.' Uncle Dick completed the list. 'All good comrades in a pinch.'

'Then don't talk about home yet,' Uncle Mogg said to him. 'We got a job to do and gostering here won't see it finished.'

Infantry habit caused them to set off from the station in patrol order. Walking in single file in the early afternoon my nine uncles were making for a long-awaited confrontation; Uncle Dick the corporal leading, then uncles Wallace, Bert, Wiley, Teddie, Tom, Fred and Billy, and the Amos brothers, Billy and Jack. Uncle Mogg sloped along in the rear, carrying his rifle at the trail.

At the Pennytown crossroads they brewed black tea in a billy, rolled a fag and laced the hot smoky fluid with

13

the last of some French brandy Uncle Wiley had been carrying in his water-bottle. Swigging out of banged enamel mugs, they took courage as they guzzled up the dregs.

Only Uncle Billy, a church sidesman and reader of the lessons, coughed at the raw spirit and thought to speak his mind.

'Are you sure we're doing the right thing, Mogg? Scripture says . .'

'Scripture says? You parson's yeoman, you!'

As Mogg's look fell upon him, eyes which had gazed unblinking through the sights to many an enemy mother's sorrow made Billy back down to a mutter.

'I . . I only thought to mention.'

'Well don't!'

The Ready Boys trudged on another half an hour till they reached their destination, a journey daily traced and relished for upwards of a year. In all that time the vow of retribution had burned in Uncle Mogg's head, full of bullets, blood and lonely murder, like a red-hot filament.

'There it is,' he told the others.

And again, more softly to himself said

'There it bliddy is!'

Aidan Hind was up a ladder at the side of Dove Cottage replacing tiles on the roof of the brew'us, the traditional small outhouse where beer was brewed for the home, washing done in the copper and the cottage pig hung from a beam after the customary November slaughter. The occupied man did not hear the click of the wicket gate – they took good care of that – nor did he turn till he sensed their presence in a group below.

'Why, er – hello, boys. Back from the War then, is it?'

'Where's that Emmy?'

Uncle Mogg had no time to waste. Not any.

'Her . . her's just gone down the village.'

'You liar!'

'Now look 'ere . .'

Aidan Hind would have started down the ladder but Mogg ripped out his bayonet with a scrape of butcher's steel.

'Another step and I'll pin you to that brew'us door.'

'We got no argument wi' thee,' said Uncle Tom the gamekeeper, who used the country form of speech. 'Best stay as thee bist. I know he'll do it, certain.'

It had all been planned so long and carefully. While the rest stood guard some of them went into the house and dragged Emmy Hind, a slovenly pig-eyed woman in a flour-sack apron, out and into the yard. The black-and-white cat just had time to bolt, scattering some timid fowls at a meal-pan, and then the vengeful men closed ranks on her preventing all escape.

Mogg unbuttoned a tunic pocket and took out his army paybook. Flipping it open he shoved a small bunch of white chicken feathers under the woman's nose.

'I been saving these. You know what they are?'

'No I don't . .'

'You wicked old sow, you sent them.'

'. . no I never,' she wailed, jowls shaking and heavy lids puckering with fright.

'Well we're informed you did, wrote to us in a letter. You sent white feathers to our Jim and Ellis, twin lads hardly in their teens, so they'd have to join the soldiers or be shamed.'

'I never . . oh, God's truth, I never.'

'God's truth?' Uncle Mogg spat back. 'God's truth is, I swore to Him you'd eat these, and I'll bliddy see you do!'

Done with words they pinioned her arms, pushed her to her knees and merciless Mogg thrust the feathers one by one into Emmy Hind's mouth, clamping her jaws shut, forcing her to swallow.

Two curved rows of little yellow shells, her false teeth,

15

came out and tumbled on the ground. Someone kicked them heartlessly away.

'Eat! Eat, and damn you!' Mogg shouted. 'And think of two green brothers, caught and cut to ribbons by the guns.'

When it was over the men retraced their steps along the cottage path. Aidan Hind came swiftly down the ladder to help his wife, still stretched and retching in the yard.

He shook his fist.

'I'll have the law on you,' he raged. 'I'm a constable in the reserve. I'll see you 'anged, the lot of you!'

It was nearly his last remark.

Tides kept quelled for long enough surged up and bludgeoned Uncle Mogg's temples, where bone and reason lie the thinnest.

At the garden gate, before anyone could stop him, he threw his rifle up and loosed a shot away. The high-velocity bullet spanged into the brew'us wall an inch from Aidan Hind's head and soft red brick dust sprayed his shoulders like a lethal bloody pollen.

'For God's sake, man!' cried Uncle Billy.

Hardened men they were, but none could foresee that Mogg would have a clip in, in readiness to fire.

Uncle Mogg was unrepentant.

'You do that, Mr Special Constable,' he mocked him, 'and see where it'll get you.'

But Aidan Hind never did –

'Hello . .'

– the prospect of death had flowered on his cheek like an angry sore –

'. . hello . .'

– and he and his wife thought better of his rashness.

'. . hello, Uncle Wallace!'

16

And there I was in front of him. Still young enough to be seen and not heard sometimes, but almost grown out of it now; wearing sandals and no socks, short summer trousers and a fawn aertex shirt my mother said was expensive but good for the skin in hot weather. And not to get it dirty on the train.

'That Mogg . .' I heard him murmur.

I could tell then what he had been thinking about, the tale I'd heard so often.

'. . he used to be a terror.'

He took off his bowler hat and fanned himself as he spoke and I burst out laughing at the lettuce leaf like a wet green wig on his head. The sound was a stone through the window of his past. Suddenly the glare of the sun and its blaring heat carried him back to now and he was once more alive and breathing shallow among the riot of green hedgerows, the tireless grasshoppers, bone-dry birds and flopping wayside flowers.

'Hello, boy!' he trumpeted. 'I never heard the train come in.'

For all his size – and there was a good six feet and twenty billowing stone of him – he slipped off the wall like a big brown circus bear and crushed me in a hug.

'Never even heard it!'

I felt my ribs go, one after the other . .

'Where's your luggage?' he demanded.

. . no more to him than twigs of wicker.

'The ticket-man said he'd send it.'

'That's all right then.'

We walked along the lane, catching up on the news, enquiring after friends and relatives and flicking the persistent sticky-footed flies from round our heads with a couple of switches from the hedge.

'Why were they called the Ready Boys of the Wrekin?' I asked.

'They used to get up groups of volunteers for the

Front, and give them names from the locality. A bit of patriotic swank, like,' said Uncle Wallace.

He sighed . .

'Twenty Boys to start with. Nine left where they lay.'

. . and we walked on a minute or two.

'Mind you,' he said. 'Auntie Fan reckons it's coming again.'

'What is?'

'Another war.'

'Is she right?'

'I wouldn't reject her opinion out of hand. She keeps writing to the papers, and she's well up in her subject.'

Further on, having a breather on a milestone, I said 'What happened to the Hinds?'

'Them? They packed their traps and left the district after that. It got about somehow, and nobody would give them time of day.'

I thought of the unsavoury couple and wondered where they were now. Then I thought of poor Uncle Mogg, buried in his uniform in a corner of the churchyard, and hoped wherever they were their every moment was a mounting burden.

★　　★　　★

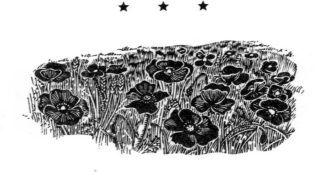

★

When we reached the spot where three lanes met we came to Trucklebed Farm. It was not a well-kept place. Gradual neglect had left it with nine toes in the grave.

Most of the outbuildings, half brick and topped with weathered clapboard, were tumbledown to say the least and the farm gate was pushed back, broken on its hinges, the brick support knocked all askew.

Out in the yard a black-skirted woman, well in her sixties, stood feeding crusts to some little flannel ducks. Stopped like a jarred clock in his head at ten when a heavy block-and-tackle fell on him in the barn, her only son, a simple-minded man of forty-odd, sat in a sagging cane chair by the porch sticking feathers in a large potato.

'Hello, Wallace,' called the woman as we came into view. 'Don't go by, will you?'

'Hello, Flossie. Hello, Gwilym.'

'Stay and have a glass of pop. I won't be half a jiffy.'

She disappeared into the house.

Gwilym looked up, thick-bodied and held in, just, by straining waistcoat buttons.

'I'm making a 'tater-hawk, see?'

Having feathered the body he was pushing longer feathers, fan-shape, into the flesh of the potato to make a tail like that of a hovering kestrel. Hung on a stick and harness thread in the garden it was supposed to keep birds from pilfering the peas and wood-pigeons from stripping down the greens.

'I'll have those dickey-birds in fits,' he told me.

And he smiled like a broken comb.

Presently Flossie came out with glasses on a tray, a plate of seed cake and a dark green bottle with the cork wired down. When she released it there was a noise like a grenade going off and the downy ducks quacked and fled in all directions.

Gwilym, his boots laced up with baling string, danced with glee and did a clumsy cartwheel in the yard.

20

We sat round munching cake, drinking dandelion pop, putting the world to rights and trying to guess how long it would be before the weather broke, with even the well-water coming up so cloudy.

Uncle Wallace could not be still for long. His eye was on the broken gate.

'Fetch me a bucket of mortar, Gwil,' he said. 'A dadderky gate I can't abide.'

Between us it didn't take long to straighten the upright somebody's muck-cart had demolished. Uncle Wallace cemented the bricks back expertly and re-set the loosened hinges.

'Leave that to dry,' he said, 'and you can hang the gate back in the morning.'

'I can pick it up like firewood,' said Gwilym.

He would have demonstrated his strength, but his mother was coming back across the yard carrying a bulging cloth bag. In it were a peck of new potatoes, swilled clean under the yard pump, a bunch of mint and a couple of summer cabbages.

'Take these home to supper,' she said. 'That gate's been an eyesore long enough.'

It was not for Uncle Wallace to refuse.

Over and again I was to see the old ways of barter and exchange in goods and services had not changed in country ages. Hard cash was not necessary and simply got in the way a lot of the time.

If you could stop a dripping tap, get the parlour clock going again, paint a front room out, plough a back piece, hang a closet door or glaze a pantry window, well, so you did. Sooner or later you would need somebody else's return of favour. And a pat of cottage butter, a bunch of flowers, a few eggs or a pull of carrots, something of what you had, was ample recompense.

That and a few fair words.

'Thank you kindly, Wallace,' said Flossie. 'We're very grateful.'

'Go on,' he said. 'You more than paid me.'

As they walked towards the road I tagged along with Gwilym. Passing the porch he picked up his 'tater-hawk.

'Here, I want you to have it.'

'What about you?'

'Oh, I can make another.'

Then he took an empty treacle tin off the window ledge.

'Look,' he said. 'See if you can do this for next time. You have to fill the tin with shouts . .'

He shouted into it and quickly put his hand over the top.

'. . and try to catch one, see? When you let your hand off the shout should come out on its own.'

Disappointment furrowed his brow when nothing happened.

'I been trying for ages,' he said sadly, 'but I just can't get the 'ang of it.'

There was a pause and then he said

'Didn't we laugh when the pop went bang?'

I had to feel sorry for him. Sorry for the accident that scrambled his brain and left it rambling in his head like an untrained rose, blooming fitfully, but never for long, in a walled garden of permanent simplicity.

At the bend of the road we turned to wave. Mother and son stood together at the new-mended gate and waved back excitedly.

'Love to Jessie,' I heard them calling.

A few minutes later we left the road in favour of a short cut to the village, through Jasper Tuck's meadow where Ossie the moony bull rattled his chain and vaguely hoped you didn't know he wouldn't hurt a fly; then along the spinney, across Restharrow and Posy Piece – fields with names older than old – up and over Steeple Spy till the church came into sight and the beginnings of the cottages.

A pound to a penny Mrs Maudie Garbett would just happen to be in the garden, seeing who was passing. It was her dedication. People said she only went indoors when it rained. Either that or she couldn't have had any chairs in the house.

We were taking turns carrying the bag and in the relentless heat its weight was making my forehead trickle.

'Phew, are these potatoes or a ton of bricks?'

'They'll weigh no more than half soon,' said Uncle Wallace.

'It beats me how they can put a station so far from the village.'

'And I'll carry the rabbits.'

'What rabbits?' I said.

Then I saw him, seated on the spinney stile, dressed in a rag overcoat and cast-off hat from the parish jumble, the ends of snares trailing from his pockets like dull copper fuses.

I didn't like the look of that unshaven foxy face nor the whiff of a briar pipe which smelt as if he was smoking shreds of his own overcoat so I wandered off and pretended to search for birds' nests; though I was close enough to know another rural transaction was taking place and to see, as the man heaved off the stile and opened his coat he was ballasted with a dozen or more dead rabbits hanging limply from his belt.

There came a snatch of conversation.

'How much?'

'Fourpence apiece, a shilling for two.'

It was the old joke but both men chuckled as the potatoes were tipped in a damp mound on the grass, divided out and handed over with a cabbage and some mint. A brace of rabbits changed hands – but no money –

after which we were left by ourselves, with just the faint suggestion of shag tobacco on the air.

Or was it burnt overcoat?

'I never saw him leave,' I said.

'No, you wouldn't,' agreed Uncle Wallace.

'Who was it?'

'Just a chap who likes to come and go.'

He didn't elaborate so I left it at that. I had enough to do coping with the vegetable bag and trying to shout into Gwilym's tin. My school reports said I was a good trier and you never knew, I might just stumble on the knack.

At the end of the church wall, saying good-day to button-booted little Grannie Higgs on her daily toddle with her cat in a carrier bag, we came to the first of the cottages in Clanetty.

Up to his eyes in a drift of snowy whiskers, the man who took his poorly horse indoors and put him by the fire in a muffler, Mr Daddy Rhys sat grinning silly in the sun and next door, sure enough, Mrs Maudie Garbett just happened to be in the garden eternally seeing who was going by. Her fat nimble fingers were plucking goose-berries from a laden bush by the sunny back wall and dropping them in her apron pocket.

'Monkton's Early Dessert,' she cried, tossing a handful of black-ripe berries into her mouth and chewing with a noise like bursting blisters.

'You can't beat them for juice. Try one,' she offered.

We dipped into her apron.

She was right . .

And again.

. . they were delicious.

'On holiday is it?' she said to me, wiping seeds off her chin. 'That's nice. It's bound to rain tomorrow!'

We stayed long enough for Uncle Wallace to promise he'd do something about the ricketty leg of her deal-top table, which had belonged to her mother when she was a Miss Owen from Llandafty and you can't get them like that now for love nor money, and even if you could, the price, you'd get a shock and that's a fact, and we were on our way again with a quart of gooseberries in Uncle Wallace's bowler hat.

'Dear me, can she tell the tale?' he said. 'No wonder her table's got a short leg!'

Pleased at the thought of rabbit pie and goosegog tart for supper, his good humour lasted through the village, across the green and up the garden path to his own front door, which adjoined the little general store he and his wife kept as a means of livelihood.

It melted there like butter in the sun.

Her broad back to us, Aunt Jessie was busy hearth-stoning the step respectable for Sunday.

Uncle Wallace crept up and slapped her playfully across the backside.

'Two pints please, Percy,' she said, without turning round.

'What?' he bellowed, instantly beside himself.

Instinctively I drew back.

'Two pints, bliddy Percy, is it?' ranted the two of him. 'If ever he lays a hand on you, I'll swing for him, I will!'

Aunt Jessie straightened up, grinning all over her face. She was big, like him. A soft motherly spread of a woman, with the most lilting voice you ever wished to hear.

'I knew it was you,' she said. 'Caught you, didn't I? Hello, boy.'

'No you never,' he tried to bluster.

'Hello, Aunt Jessie,' I said.

'Yes I did,' she said. 'I saw you coming up the lane five minutes ago. How was the journey?'

'No you never,' he said again.

'Not bad,' I answered, wondering what I was doing in the conversation at all.

'After all this time,' Aunt Jessie murmured fondly. 'Who's still jealous then?'

'And isn't there a reason . .'

'Who is?' she honeyed him.

'. . when a man can't hardly turn around . .'

'Tell me?'

Her cadences were pure delight.

'. . not for a minute . .'

'I want to know.'

'. . but what his wife is being slapped saucy by every Tom, Dick and bliddy milkman?'

Aunt Jessie simply waited until . .

'I am,' he had to admit in the end.

Looking sheepishly down and kicking up the ground, the last of his bluster vanished into thin air like a wisp of steam from the *Princess Alice*.

'Oh, there's better now.'

Satisfied Aunt Jessie rewarded him with a kiss. Big as he was she could wrap him round her little finger.

It was my turn to toe the ground. I felt like a peeping-tom.

'Don't mind us, love,' said Aunt Jessie cheerfully, giving me a kiss also. 'Life is a lovely battle, when you've got the right man to make a scrap of it with. And I've got one in a million! How long are you staying?'

'A year,' I said, 'or thereabouts.'

I must say Aunt Jessie took it in her stride.

'Didn't you get the letter?'

'Letter? We only got a postcard, to say that you were coming.'

At the responsibility of having to sentence somebody to a year of me I withdrew some of my outer perimeters, trying to look smaller, more like an orphan, under my clothes. But then again, having no children of their own – why, I didn't know – I thought Uncle Wallace and Aunt

Jessie might be content to have the tiny attic bedroom lived in for a while.

Occupation is good for a room lain idle; it pushes back the damp behind the wallpaper. Perched up among the clean rain-washed Welsh slates at the top of the house, a stone's throw from the crisp cold stars and swaying in the winds of March and October gales like a rook's nest up a tree, it had been empty far too long.

Inwardly Aunt Jessie could hide the sorrow of her earlier barren years, but when it did show on her face she said it was nothing to bother about. Just a bit tired, that's all. On her worst days it was a tragedy; at best a poignant reminder that things worked out only some of the time.

Beyond that, life was what you made it.

As for me . .

In some complication of circumstances at home, due to my father changing jobs, moving house by fifty miles, fixing up the new one and making it habitable after the herd of elephants my mother said must have been living there, they thought it preferable – another way of saying I was not to be consulted – if I was sent off to the country for a while.

I didn't mind their odd decision. Little did they know, I would have settled for Tibet and Samarkand at any time.

I opened my mouth to start explaining and closed it again, for in the meantime Percy Pugh's milk cart had drawn up in a slither of hooves and the dull bim-bom of colliding milk churns. I quickly excused myself and said I ought to go and say hello to all the neighbours. Then curiosity got the better of me and I hid down the lane, just within earshot.

Not a minute went by before an affronted milkman was leaping back into his cart.

'You're mad,' he cried. 'Mad as a bliddy hatter. As if I would. Me, who's on the parish council!'

'There's no smoke . .' came the reply.

'It only takes two signatures on a committal order.'

'. . not without fire.'

'And I'll sign yours twice!'

'I told you I knew it was you,' Aunt Jessie kept saying.

All to no avail.

'Anyway . .'

With his parting shot Percy Pugh unleashed a bulls-eye.

'. . how can I take seriously the threats of a man who stands there wearing a bliddy lettuce leaf instead of a hat?'

His Woodbine a glowing squib, he snatched up his whip and drove away like a charioteer.

'Why didn't you tell me?' I heard Uncle Wallace growl.

'I thought you knew.'

Then came a chuckle.

'Did you really know it was me, honest?'

'Course I did, you great softie!'

'Oh dear, what'll we do for milk now?'

As for me again . .

By now I was light-headed.

A victim of the sun and circumstance, feeling daft by contagion from cake and cartwheels, cats in carriers, a horse in the house, goosegogs, wobbly tables and aireated milkmen wrongfully indicted, shouting into Gwilym's tin with the exultation of a lunatic given a popgun and told to shoot down all the stars, I made off down the lane in raptures.

Success was not important. The joy lay in the trying.

★3★

★

Bake a tansy pudding . . graft an apple tree . . trim a head of hair, properly mind, not round a basin . . mend a china dog . . pull a tooth, the good old-fashioned way . .

I had drifted off to sleep listing ways of lending a hand in Clanetty and woke up with my finger probing my mouth looking for the molar I dreamt was about to be extracted by the string-and-doorknob method of country story.

It was no Indian rope-trick. I had seen it done a couple of times.

The expectation of sharp and sudden pain brought me awake better than any alarm clock. I opened my eyes. Above me was the bowed contour of the attic bedroom ceiling, bellying down comfortably like the hull of an old boat, done over mostly white, except where Uncle Wallace had run out of paper and had to finish the strip nearest the hearth with half a roll of pale blue stripes and pink roses left over from when he did the pantry out.

Realising where I was, an incoming wave of lazy bliss broke over me like the warm careening of the sea. Then a rooster announced the morning from somebody's orchard near by. Still-tired hens were meeting in moody clusters to mew and scratch for breakfast under the apple-coming boughs and as the sun yawned awake rubbing sleep from its eyes I was summoned out of bed by a powerful force, unknown to me in towns.

Sliding barefoot across polished brown lino slick as tray-toffee I poked my head out of the casement window and looked upon the land.

In one uninterrupted view I breathed in all the valley, seeing the mercury ribbon of Evensong brook, full of the lively dace and fat little trout the Reverend Powys could never seem to catch, then the near fields and the far, until a drifting early mist obscured the detail and washed up to the first low line of hills. These blended into the bluer body of middle-distance hills, none of whose ancient musical names I could recall, and they matched in turn with the furthest and highest range rumpled along the skyline like the pushed-back eiderdown at the bottom of the bed.

The tapering ends of Shropshire eased imperceptibly into the first-footings of Wales, fading out and into one another through delft-blue and delphinium to far-off slopes of purple, the colour of mountain stormclouds, with neither delineation nor divide, no hindrance to the eye nor curb to the imagination.

To this private and unrivalled outlook I would return again and again, hunched on the creaky box seat, chin in hands, when I wanted to be alone or have a think. In time it became my sanctum and my solace, almost my sole right and jealously guarded possession. Other eyes might now and then look from my window but they could not, nor could they ever, see what only I could see.

Remote and far and beckoning, this rightly was . . The Land.

When its inhabitants spoke of it you heard their vocal emphasis, and thus their pride belonging. Solitary, spiritual, clear of air, crystal-springed and manna-mossed, fairy-delled in the lower places, the stamping-ground of stag-legged natural gods who lived and foraged in the high; elusively peopled by aerial beings not seen but felt by intuition; a magical, mystic province, it lay as it would always lie, strumming its own repeating fable on the harp of the winds for as long as forever is.

It lies there now, if you know the trick of looking.

As I pulled on my clothes, hurrying to be out and about in the available magic, I heard some blithe soul on the way down the garden to the earth-closet at the far end sing the first verse of Cwm Rhondda and I realised it was Sunday.

There came the snap of the backyard hasp door and

Uncle Wallace was joining in. A third voice added itself, and a fourth, and from the four closets huddled in a square overgrown with wild honeysuckle at the bottoms of the adjacent gardens I was treated to the sound of a male-voice quartet moved by music and the call of morning regularity.

Better than the wireless they gave me, and anyone else who wanted to listen, the rest of 'Guide Me, O thou great Redeemer', two revival hymns – 'My Mother's Bible' and 'Come on the Wings of the Morning' – something catchy I couldn't place just then, most likely Gilbert and Sullivan, and rounded off with Parry's 'Jerusalem'.

It was a spirited start to the day.

After breakfast . .

'How did you sleep?'

'Like a top.'

'Are you hungry?'

'Falling through myself.'

'Well, there's eggs and streaky bacon, a bit of flash-in-the-pan, black pudding, fried bread, and toast and my slab-marmalade.'

'Yes please!'

'What, all of it?'

Aunt Jessie jostled the gantry pan and stood aside to let the fat splash.

'You'll be the size of *him* if you're not careful.'

. . after breakfast I took a turn around the garden.

They said he was no gardener, the old dads, shaking their hoary heads, full of tips and know-how, and Uncle Wallace listened patiently, putting his round open face and minimum of features to good account as they criticised, tapped the sides of their noses and offered him the benefit of experience and the seasons' lore.

You'll have no luck with those . .

No, I expect you're right, he said, in due course pulling up turnips like bunches of babies' heads.

. . nor those . .

I don't suppose so, he puffed, having to tug-o'-war the carrots out of the ground, they bedded down so far.

. . and you'll get no sweet peas to speak of neither.

Sure to be true, he answered, garnering fragrant armfuls like pastel summer butterflies on long slender stalks, enough for all the vases in the house.

He also raised marrows like striped zeppelins and literally lugged the pumpkins away one at a time in a barrow to the cellar, ready-made bright orange carboys for his potent pumpkin rum, a treat in store for Christmas.

In the end they left him to it, the meddlers. Blinking rheumily, like aged barn owls caught in the light, they doddered off down the pub, tapped their dottle and muttered as they hugged consoling pints.

Well, he gets away with it, granted, but nobody can tell him anything!

Indoors, getting ready for church, Aunt Jessie was trying to do something with my hair when the telephone rang behind the counter in the shop.

Uncle Wallace rumbled away to answer it.

In its dark-varnished box, with a little shelf for writing messages, it was fixed on the wall amid a dangling miscellany of cards of liver pills, corn-and-wart solvent, Daisy headache powders, bunion pads and ointment for chapped hands. An object of suspicion and distrust, bawled down awkwardly and with some embarrassment, it was unnecessary for regular and passing customers but essential for what Uncle Wallace referred to as the carriage end of the trade.

Local gentry, people like the squire, the doctor, and Miss Florence up at the Big House preferred to place their weekly orders that way and have them delivered in Uncle

Wallace's oval-windowed van. It gave them the sense of separation they needed and underlined the setting apart of the privileged classes from the rest of humanity.

'Tck, your hair's like Heaven,' said Aunt Jessie, running it through with a watered comb. 'There *is* no parting!'

She was still trying and getting nowhere when Uncle Wallace came back.

'Who was it?'

'Our Dick. Millie's calling for us to go to church.'

'Well she always does, doesn't she?'

'I know,' said Uncle Wallace, 'but I think he likes to warn us just the same.'

In the distance the church bells had already begun to ring by the time Aunt Millie arrived. As soon as she saw me her face took a turn for the worst.

'Hello, boy,' she said, with no enthusiasm whatsoever.

'Hello, Aunt Millie.'

'On holiday are we?'

'Yes, Aunt Millie,' I said. 'I like your Sunday hat.'

'Hmm . .!'

Again she looked at me like something that had gone off in the larder.

'No more rude recitals, not this time, I hope?'

'No, Aunt Millie.'

So be it.

She would never let me forget the cause of our grudging relationship, I decided, as I replied politely and bit my tongue in two places.

I was six when it happened, one Sunday, on a day's visit. How proud I was of my first year at school and of the things I learned both in and out of classroom.

As we sat round at the formal gathering of high tea – my mother and father, Uncle Wallace and Aunt Jessie, Uncle Dick and Aunt Millie and one or two of her friends from the church Ladies' Committee – where I was generally overlooked, in a gap in the conversation I was suddenly invited to say something.

I told them about being made monitor and allowed to give out slates and pencils; about singing 'Jesus wants me for a sunbeam', solo and word-perfect at morning assembly, and then the games we played at playtime after we had drunk our ha'penny bottle of milk in the infants' cloakroom.

A chatterbox of a boy even then, I loved being the centre of attention.

'We play hide-and-seek,' I told my audience, 'and "tick" as well. They always let me do the count-me-out.'

'The count-me-out?' said Aunt Millie indulgently. 'Whatever can that be?'

'It's a rhyme you say, and point at everybody till you reach the last, and they're "it",' I explained, 'for that game. Shall I say one?'

They nodded their assent.

'Nebuchadnezzar, the king of the Jews,
Sold his wife for a pair of shoes,
When the shoes began to wear,
Nebuchadnezzar began to swear.'

They shouldn't have laughed and led me on. I stood on my chair and gave them another.

'The Lord said unto Moses,
"Your tribe shall have big noses,
Excepting poor old Aaron
And he shall have a square one"!'

At the next round of applause and obvious delight I was in my element. I was loved. I was wanted. I was a universal success. The spotlight was on me, the diminutive six-year-old usually forgotten about, told to be quiet or keep his elbows off the table, and the show-off in me wasn't going to let it dwindle now.

So I gave them my best piece for an encore.

'Ike said to Mike
"Can your mother ride a bike
With her arm in a sling
And her finger up her thing
And a bell on her arse
That goes ting-a-ling-a-ling?" '

In that moment the church Ladies' Committee turned into a group of statuary. My mother and father appeared to have disowned me and Uncle Dick stared holes in the tablecloth, cherry-eared and blowing his nose like a euphonium. Aunt Jessie, not knowing where to put herself, bit her finger half-through and had a good mind to have hysterics.

No other sound broke the awesome silence save that of Uncle Wallace, who had managed to stagger out to the back kitchen in the throes of some sort of fit which he attempted to smother by burying his face in the roller-towel behind the door.

'Another cup of tea, anybody?' said Aunt Jessie, in somebody else's voice.

The pot was so put out the lid jumped up and sputtered.

Then, out of shock and silence, came consternation and a rush of action.

My mother, forced to make a gesture, smacked me on the legs and called me a downright shameful wicked naughty boy, and said not to look for my Saturday penny ever again.

I ran howling into the back kitchen where the outraged church committee, headed by Aunt Millie with uprolled sleeves and bar of soap already in her hand, insisted they had never heard such words and couldn't wait to wash my mouth out.

To his lasting credit Uncle Wallace, emerging from the roller-towel, would have none of it.

'Oh no you don't. Not in my house,' he said. 'Now go back in the parlour, there's good ladies, while I take *him* . .' He aimed a thumb at me. '. . down the garden and give him a good telling-off.'

'Telling-off? I know what *I'*d do. I'd turn his trousers down . .'

'. . and tan his little bottom . .'

'. . with a big long cane!'

'Well, we'll see,' said Uncle Wallace.

Instead he steered me, by the ear for the sake of appearances, to a cast-iron bench between the rhubarb and the redcurrants, pushed a toffee in my mouth when it opened to howl again and pointed out the folly of parroting words I didn't know the meaning of, especially rude ones.

Then he gave me a shilling which he took back immediately and replaced with a florin.

'Here! I haven't laughed so much for ages,' he said. 'Only not a word to *them*, mind!'

I didn't intend one.

At such a tender age, calf-like and putting all my trust in them, I was already vowing I would never be led astray by sly grown-ups again.

Coming up the churchyard path we were joyously harried by the morning peal of bells, giving tongue as eager as a pack of hounds, and from a June bride's wedding just the other day strewn confetti blew like blossom on the path.

The belfry birds had pecked up all the rice.

As we stood talking at the porch where the Reverend Powys, alongside the verger, Mr Popelady, greeted every parishioner with the same Christian amiability, a selection of my uncles and aunts began to turn up; Uncle Fred, Uncle Tom and Uncle Teddie, accompanying their wives, respectively, Aunts Tilly, Vinnie and Daisy May.

Without exception they all said

'Hello, boy.'

It seemed the standard form of greeting when they met me; one on which they all agreed. I hardly ever heard my own name till Laylie came to say it, that once and only once, but it made me grateful for the omission until then. The way she used it, at that time and in that place, meant she had secured it, for safekeeping or disposal as she wished; and if she forgot, she knew I would remember.

It was time to go into the service.

Mr Handel Daniels, the organist, was bringing his morning voluntary to a close and in addition we could all see Miss Florence's carriage, gleaming enamelled black and gold, just drawn up by Brown her manservant under the magnificent horse-chestnut by the church gates.

It was her custom, as quite the most important person locally and a generous benefactor of the church, to arrive at and enter it last. Also to have the Reverend Powys escort her up the path and see her to her pew.

Brown, a practising imbiber and non-churchgoer, would wait beneath the mantling shade of the best conker tree for miles and take frequent nips from a silver flask until it was time to drive back to the Big House, often under the weather and sometimes nearly under the seat.

I thought, if I pull my shoelace undone and take my time tying it . .

'Where have you been?' whispered Aunt Jessie when I joined them quietly, seventh pew down, right-hand side.

'I waited to say hello to Miss Florence.'

'I thought you'd got lost.'

'She invited me to tea,' I told her. 'A month today. She wrote it in her diary.'

'Well now, I'll tell *you* something,' said Aunt Jessie. 'It slipped my mind till now.'

'What did?'

'There's no school Monday,' she said, 'and none till next September. They're having to redecorate and build another classroom, so everybody's got an extra holiday, including you!'

People were turning round to look, I sang the opening hymn so loud.

★ ★ ★

★ **4** ★

★

After that arriving weekend I settled in like a duck takes to water, happy to receive a weekly letter from my mother and becoming part of the landscape outside, part of the furniture in.

Now thoroughly aired of its emptiness, where at first it had been none too pleased at the intrusion, my room gradually took a liking to me, though I was conscious of a period, a few days, of probation before the powers unseen relented.

Moreover, when impersonal, familiarity breeds content, and soon the wallpaper warmed and became responsive, the fabrics of the room accommodating when I returned and aimed my untidy boy's imprint at baggy-bottomed sofa or bed, and the influence all round – which I could sometimes discern in the night as real and shimmering as gossamer on my face – a guarding, guiding one.

I was sure whoever had lived in the house before was still there, up among the slates and stars, and wanted me to know their presence would be one of comfort. Undecided whether or not to communicate yet, someone was definitely watching over me.

I would have to ask Aunt Belle, Uncle Joss's wife, about that when I saw her.

On an earthier level altogether, peony-cheeked and comely, Aunt Jessie was full of happiness to have me in the house. She sang about her work, operatic in the open air, more mutedly melodious in the parlour, plying her duster with a will and frequently giving me impulsive hugs for no other reason than knowing she had only to reach out and enfold me.

And always it was such a fond embrace; an outpouring of herself which left me warm as done toast.

'You'll be a bit of company for me in the evenings,' she said, 'when his lordship goes off to the pub.'

'What about Billingsgate?'

'Useless,' said Aunt Jessie. 'He's out on the tiles from dusk to dawn.'

'Well there's always Auntie Fan.'

'Tucked up tight and fast asleep by eight o'clock!'

'I see what you mean,' I said.

There was no denying it. Billingsgate, Uncle Wallace's tomcat, was a law unto himself and came and went as he pleased. Barrel-chested and boxing-glove-pawed, fiercely whiskered and with chisel eyes that made you shiver, he could make mincemeat out of anything below the size of a Shetland pony. The yellow bulldog down the road was terrified and fell on his back grinning like an imbecile at Billy's mere approach.

Concerning Auntie Fan, who helped in the shop and lived in the cupboard under the stairs, Aunt Jessie was right again. Elderly, nimble as a cricket and seeming to exist on a diet of sugared pobs and hot sweet tea, she kept herself to herself, made a huge pitcher of bread-and-milk every night for supper and retired among her bits and bobs and tranklements until it was time to sink her teeth and whistle out the candle at a quarter to the hour on the dot.

Swathed in a red-flannel nightie, lace-capped in summer, fleece-bedsocked in winter, all night long she snored in the airless cupboard like a wasp in a bottle and appeared to thrive on it.

'Besides, he's a cat. I can't talk to him,' went on Aunt Jessie. 'Not and get a sensible reply. And I don't know anything about politics.'

'Even if Auntie Fan did sit up?' I said.

'Quite!'

The timetable of my days was beginning to take shape. The school board had chosen the right time of year for its refurbishing programme. Attendance in the summer months was patchy, according to demands of crop and weather, with understood absence more the order of the day. Education could wait; setting out the cabbages wouldn't: it was as simple as that. Family pairs of hands, however small, could be put to more profitable use on the land.

After the formative years of getting what they could out of the three Rs, clever heads and dunces alike, almost all would come to that, rising no higher, nor wanting to, anyway.

In the meantime the countryside – field, farm, roadside cottage plot and garden – made further demands on book-learning by taking back the juvenile population periodically to help with picking the produce, hoeing and weeding, re-planting and bird-scaring, whatever task the never-ending cycle of the rotating earth deemed next in line.

If there was a fourth R it was repetition, with no hope of the fifth, remission.

All well and good if you enjoyed it; life was a merry-go-round: if not, it was your treadmill and your daily grind.

With no local ties nor obligations I was under no such sentence. I spent blissful mornings in the shop, learning the tricks of the trade till I could carve cheese with the wire into masterpieces of gold and yellow solid geometry, bag the demerara, trickle loose tea into hand-made packets, shovel up the rice and bullet sago, wrap, tie and tot up the purchases, operate the brass cathedral of a till and hand out change with a professional flourish.

Trade was generally brisk and kept Auntie Fan and me on the go, but in slack moments we bowled up a couple of Cheddar cheeses and sat back of the counter sharing our shop assistants' perks, dropped jam tarts, the ends of the Dundee cake slabs, snips of cheese, trimmings of boiled ham off the bone and broken biscuits in bewildering variety from the racks of big square manufacturers' tins with the glass tops.

In the middle of the afternoon Aunt Jessie often joined us with a pot of tea for three which became four or five or six if customers happened back for something they'd forgotten.

One afternoon we had just sat down as usual when Mrs Lily Prospero, the policeman's wife from Clett, came in for a jar of Volcano Paste for her husband's sciatica back.

It was a day when we were doing particularly well for cakes. Auntie Fan, going up the shop ladder earlier, missed a rung on the way down and landed on a put-by box of macaroons, madeleines and almond slices. With a dozen or more squashed fancies to get rid of, Aunt Jessie asked Mrs Prospero to stay for tea.

A bossy, gossipy little woman with beetroot cheeks, a nose that glowed like a whitlow, friendly false teeth and a silver Mizpah brooch, Mrs Prospero had always had a fatal attraction for me.

Because Mrs Prospero had been to hospital and had had . . Everything Taken Away.

I happened to overhear granny saying so once to Uncle Teddie's wife and from then on I never ceased to stare at her in thoughtful speculation.

Outwardly she still retained her faculties and the use of all her limbs, so what had been Taken Away, and so sweepingly? Had they ethered her into a deep and dreamless slumber, opened her up from neck to navel, removed every internal organ and stitched her up again with catgut, tight as a football lace and neat as a pair of granny's stays?

If so, what awful cavity remained, and when she ate did every mouthful fall down inside like a stone down a mineshaft till it reached the bottom with a dull resounding thud? Or an echoing splash if she was full of tea?

Fascinated anew I was staring now, my cheeks drawn fine as vellum.

Suddenly aware of my eyes so fixed upon her – to the exclusion of everything else – as to appear disembodied, Mrs Prospero worried her brooch and checked her tittle-tattle.

'Is there . . something wrong with me, my lad . . or something wrong with you?'

'Oh no, Mrs Prospero,' I said hastily. 'I er – I like your new hat.'

'I like your new hat' – new hat, Sunday hat, red, blue or straw hat, described as met the case – was one of my disarming lines when faced with difficult ladies. It was not an original device. I had copied it from Mr Grover Wheelkins, a foolish young curate always in Victorian drawing-room trouble with young women and their chaperones, in a book I read when I was ten and which made me laugh till I was eleven. He employed it with telling effect, and after him, so did I. It never failed, except in one recurring instance, and even Mr Grover Wheelkins, for all his cloth and calling, would have had trouble with Aunt Millie.

'It's very becoming,' I said to Mrs Prospero, and threw in the curate's winning smile for good measure.

'Oh-h . . becoming!' she exclaimed, all at once quite taken with me. 'It's as much as I can do to get a civil word out of *my* three. *And* their dad's a bobby!'

At that the shop bell tinkled and Uncle Will came in for his regular ounce of twist, a tin of Pirate's Trunkdust and also looking for me.

He was just off birds' nesting.

'Dost want to come?'

I looked over at Aunt Jessie.

'Go on,' she smiled. 'Make yourself scarce if you want to.'

I did want to, but at the same time there was a strong case for refusing. Thud or splash, I was on the brink of solving some of Mrs Prospero's inner mysteries. She was about to bite her almond slice when Uncle Will arrived.

45

I hesitated a moment.

On the other hand Uncle Will had a nose for a nest in the hedgebank, especially pheasants' and partridge, like a terrier for rats in the straw.

'Bist coming or bisner?'

Then regretfully shelving Mrs Prospero for another time, I hung up my green baize apron between the mole traps and the bristle brooms, helped myself to a macaroon, and went.

★ ★

Keeping my bedroom window squarely at our backs we set off westward into the valley, following the direction of Evensong brook.

All in all, he and Uncle Ben being really my great-uncles since they were great-granny's sons, Uncle Will would have been my first choice as a diverse and interesting character.

Spring-heeled and agile he could jump in and out of a barrel without touching the sides and won many a half-crown from strangers to the district doing so. As a hobby he kept a flag-day book in which were pinned numerous examples to bring out and wear on the particular Saturday, spoken of nothing but well for his apparent annual generosity, and on a fine gnat-dancing evening he would sit in the door of the woodshed and play the musical saw like an artist.

Quartering the grainfields, sturdy oats and barley, all of it coming along nicely in a prolonged spell of good growing weather, our route was taking us round every side so as not to miss any of the headlands, thick with unscythed grass and thistles, where the best game nests were bound to be.

Living well up to his reputation Uncle Will found nest after nest, more often than not putting up the sitting bird almost from under his feet with a heart-jolting whirr of

46

wings and feathers. Soon possessed of what he came for
– a couple of dozen pheasants' eggs, and some partridges',
enough for a few breakfasts – we turned for Evensong
meadow and home.

It was to prove a turn back to unexpected adventure,
mishap and wonderful windfall.

In a long-past thaw and flood, near the top of the
broad watermeadow that led homewards, the frozen winter brook which became a temporary but ungovernable
spring torrent had scoured out a sizeable pocket of red
sandy earth on either bank, leaving a deep lagoon some
forty feet across, reed-fringed and dotted round with
pollard willows.

On the way, Uncle Will pulled up short and pointed.

'There she goes, look thee.'

His quick eye had seen the mother coot, at our
approach, steal silently off a pile of dead water herbage on
a broken oak limb brought down by another surge of
water, and he knew she had a nest there, almost in the
middle of the pool.

'Hast got a dandy-coot's?'

'No, Uncle Will.'

He had only to crawl out to it and I would have
another addition to the peewit's and the snipe's already
in my egg-collecting tin.

With never a thought of danger he began to pick his
way along the branch. No sooner was he within arm's
length of the clutch of eggs, reaching out to take one, than
the whole limb rolled over, treacherous as an alligator in
the water, and plunged Uncle Will in headlong.

He should have been none the worse for his wetting,
but a few days later, when they had to get assistance in
the night . .

'Pneumonia,' said Doctor Colley-Jones, precise in his
instructions. 'Gamgee tissue over the chest, and hot
linseed poultices. Thin soup, as much as he wants, for

nourishment. Take turn and turn about with him and call me if there's any change.'

Two days afterwards, in the late afternoon, came the crisis all were dreading.

They heard Uncle Will in his hallucinations, as in a journey to another realm, seeing his long-dead father doffing his hat at the gate, and realized then it was only a matter of hours, one way or another.

When the first hint of daylight lightened the cut panes of night in the downstairs kitchen windows Aunt Jessie, come along to help, stirred in Uncle Ben's rocking-chair and heard great-granny calling.

'Jessie . . our Ben . . come up quickly, do!'

Up they went to find the news was promising. Weak as he looked on the pillow Uncle Will had fought his duel bravely and rising dawn was heralding the day with signs of some recovery.

Two days afterwards the second crisis came, announcing itself by a sharp intimidating crack on the front door with the handle of an owl's-head brolly. Answering it, Uncle Ben stepped back with such a start they could see his expression through the back of his neck.

'Don't look so dumbstruck!' rasped Cousin Dora, rough-tongued as a file. 'I've only come to pay respects to poor dear Will. Before he passes on.'

An obscure relative from a branch of the family we didn't hold with anyway, she swept past Uncle Ben into the kitchen, skirts spitting, and sat down stiff as buckram.

'Unless of course, after coming all the way from Meredith Vale, you refuse to let me see him.'

'Poor dear Will?' whispered Uncle Ben.

Slipping off his boots and following the two women upstairs he caught Aunt Jessie on the landing as she came out of Uncle Will's room.

'Her's up to summat, mark my words.'

Pressed against the door they heard the scrape of a chair over lino and Cousin Dora thump her bag down on the floor.

'Oh Will, thank the Lord I'm not too late.'

'Too late?'

'And not to see you at the last . .'

Resting and not expecting visitors Uncle Will pulled the bedclothes up in a protective bunch as she sat beside the bed.

'At the last?' he said. 'They . . they told me I'm improving.'

'Dear, brave Will,' sighed Cousin Dora.

As though that was how she would always think of him.

She glanced down at hands generous with knuckles before continuing, hoping – despite a thorough run-through on the bus-ride over the hills – her speech would not appear too pat and practised.

'When our time is nigh, when we leave our loved ones grieving, the empty place is often hard to fill. But there's always something we can give to others, as a keepsake . .'

'So that's it!'

Feeling Uncle Ben's temper boil and rise, Aunt Jessie placed a restraining hand on his shoulder on the other side of the door.

'. . and what I'd like from you, dear Will,' said Cousin Dora, 'is that pair of china lions grandma Harriet Ann left you when she died. They're on the downstairs chimney-piece, I see. "If our Will never finds them useful" – now didn't she used to say? – "they might as well be Dora's when he's gone." '

'But I haven't gone yet,' protested Uncle Will.

'No, dear Will,' said Cousin Dora sympathetically, 'but seeing as I'm visiting, and you the way you are . .'

*

They talked about it in the village a long time after, Uncle Ben chasing Cousin Dora out of the house and down the lane in stockinged-feet, waving his old double-barrelled duckbuster and threatening to put paid to all her mischief.

When he returned eventually Uncle Will said

'Ben, I've been thinking. Go down and fetch me up the lions.'

His brother did as he was bid, and came back with them cradled in his arms. A tawny caramel colour they stood at bay on rectangular plinths, each with a forepaw resting on a sphere.

'Now take the poker,' said Uncle Will calmly, 'and knock them both to smithers in the fireplace.'

They could hardly believe their ears.

'Now, Will,' they said anxiously. 'Now then, our Will.'

'You can go on till the cows come home . .' said Uncle Will.

He took a pinch of Pirate's Trunkdust, his favourite snuff.

'. . but I'll see she never gets 'em now!'

Uncle Ben placed the Staffordshire lions, always cumbersome and heavy, in the wide slate hearth. A look at Uncle Will and a chance to change his mind then he hit one resolutely with the stout brass poker. The brittle china flew to fragments, spattering against the fender and leaving a hard moulded lump like suet lying in the debris.

'Well that's peculiar,' he said, leaning forward. 'They never used to cast . . oh-h!' He gave a gasp. 'It . . it's money!'

Cured by a miracle Uncle Will shot out of bed like a buttered ghost.

'It's a lot of old tallow, and . . and . .'

'And what?' dithered Uncle Will.

'Sovereigns,' said Uncle Ben. 'A mint of golden sovereigns.'

'Give me the poker, quick!'

Uncle Will whacked the other lion over the head and broke it open.

It contained an identical lump.

Regardless of the mess, he and Uncle Ben, great-granny and Aunt Jessie sat down to count the fortune, crumbling the perished tallow between their fingers and placing the gleaming hoard in the centre of the bed. When the final count was made there were three hundred and five sovereigns all told, and a pair of half-sovereigns.

Uncle Ben picked up the underpart of the second lion where the cast-hole remained undamaged. A coin he tried just slipped inside.

'This must have been grandma Harriet's bank. She stuck the money in with candlefat to stop it rattling,' he guessed.

'My windfall and inheritance,' murmured Uncle Will, all misty-eyed. 'Up there on the mantel and I never knew.'

'And who do you think figured that out,' said Aunt Jessie, 'and schemed her chance to get it?'

It was a question needing no reply.

Inside a week Uncle Will was fit as a flea and jumped in and out of the raintub to prove it. The soft notes of his musical saw were heard again from the woodshed and he spread the burden of his riches by splitting the three hundred sovereigns a hundred even between himself, Uncle Ben and great-granny.

In the days when a ten-bob note was a lot of money and the best of a week's backbreak for some, Aunt Jessie felt like an heiress when he made her a present of the odd five sovereigns for helping nurse him better.

'And give these the boy for his eye-money,' he said. 'If I hadn't gone after that coot's egg, none of this would have happened.'

'What's eye-money?' I said.

51

Later, when Aunt Jessie, thrilled to bits, was going over it for the umpteenth time and I was still examining my two half-sovereigns, richer than I'd ever been:

'All being well you won't be needing it,' she told me. 'At least not yet awhile.'

★　★　★

★ 5 ★

★

St Swithin's turned into the sort of day when mirrors all went hazy and you could write your name in the bloom on the polished table-top in the sitting-room.

Idly played on the venerable walnut piano, middle C dropped like a semibreve made of lead, causing upsets in its tinny innards, and now, with the change in the weather making weekend prospects hot and humid, waiting for the dog-cart to take me up to the Big House for Sunday tea, when I looked their way the jaundiced ivory keys grinned back at me like a horse over a hedge.

I was in no mood for fraternity.

Even indoors, air the consistency of sea-fret pressed on my face as steamy as a bath-night flannel and the leaves of the aspidistra, shined bottle-green every Monday fortnight by Aunt Jessie with a rag dipped in milk, displayed a marked lack of interest in anything and everything.

Including me, hemmed in and half-suffocated by my new long trousers.

'That aspidistra always looks how I feel in this weather,' said Aunt Jessie.

'The piano's out of tune,' I complained.

Aunt Jessie carried on winding her ball of wool from a skein stretched across the back of a chair.

'Mrs Patty Pritchard handed me that over the church-yard wall the day I got married and I've had it ever since. Money wouldn't buy it. She's gone now, poor old soul. Dead of a fit in the garden privy.'

'And the loud pedal doesn't work either!'

'They look very nice. Very smart and grown-up,' said Aunt Jessie encouragingly, wise as to why I was out of sorts.

Inside I groaned.

Looking grown-up was the last thing I wanted to be told; the very idea made me a rebel down to my shoes.

Short-trousered, let off the leash, led on by a boy's-eye vision dangling before me like a donkey's carrot, I wanted to traipse and trespass the patchwork fields and wildwood in a spent lifetime of high summer and Sirius dog days, making fires, damming streams, outrunning the pursuit of bow-legged farmers, scampering among cudding cows stood tickle-deep in the marshy meadows, breasting land-oceans of rippling corn or hallooing harebrained up and down the switchback hills, frolicking to my heart's content in the whim of the wayward wind.

Above all evading as long as ever I could the eventual entrapment of girls, going steady and getting spliced; then the rent, rates and humdrum responsibilities which long trousers, to me, represented the first and irrevocable step towards.

'I don't know what you're worrying about,' said Aunt Jessie, interrupting my improbable dream. 'Oh, there's the cart at the door now . .'

I gave her a kiss and took myself off.

Over tea I brightened up considerably.

The drawing-room of Miss Florence's country mansion was a sight to behold. In the tall-ceilinged room, amid her lovingly looked-after furniture, gilt-framed portraits in oil, silk cushions and displays of valuable china, there was no hint at all of an ongoing world. Neither the passing of the common hours. Only a sense of being. The permanency of as it was and shall be.

Clear, refined and held in place for a family's assured continuance, it was like a room preserved in aspic.

Supervised by Brown and served by Charlotte the maid we had tea from Coalport cups and began with love-biscuits, quaintly made to be eaten between wafery slices of home-made bread and butter, followed by pieces of delicious bible cake. I had never tasted anything so mouth-watering; it would have prompted an atheist into second thoughts.

From somewhere near the firescreen Brown coughed

a discreet reminder when I forgot myself and reached for yet another slice.

Rescuing me with graceful charm Miss Florence chuckled.

'Isn't it irresistible? I do believe I'll have another piece myself.'

For once sober and definitely not himself Brown breathed out and retired again into the background. An intense and irritable man, growing through the top of his hair with worry, he had come to the Big House many years ago to re-design the formal gardens but somehow, usually drunk beneath the rhododendrons – his fondness for drink earned him the nickname Incapability Brown – had never got round to finishing the job.

Staying on and on, original purpose forgotten, he gradually became absorbed into the everyday household and against the odds had proved his worth, not so much as landscape gardener as with his surprising flair for management of the big estate.

Village gossip being what it was I had heard there existed between him and his employer the same relationship as that once rumoured between Queen Victoria and another Brown. I found that hard to believe. Miss Florence was far too cultivated and reserved.

At eleven o'clock each weekday morning she took a glass of sherry with a dry Aviemore biscuit and attended to her correspondence. At one she ate a light luncheon, at two-thirty retired for a little nap, at three-thirty did the rounds of the garden or chatted with the head gardener in the conservatory if it was raining, and always came in to tea on the stroke of four.

Knowing she considered the ordering of the day essential and punctuality the proper compliment to an invitation I recognized also there would be a correct time for departure. It was five o'clock. I did not have to be told. Without being abrupt or glancing at the clock Miss

Florence folded her napkin delicately and said well now, wasn't that nice, she had enjoyed it and I must come again, mustn't I?

'I'll let you have the recipe for the bible cake,' she promised. 'Cook found it in an old parish magazine.'

Driving home to Clanetty, Brown let me handle the reins on the straighter parts.

'She's a nice lady, Miss Florence, isn't she?' I said.

'She's been very good to me, considering.'

'Has she any family left at all?'

'Only her brother Horrie. Lives in Bristol.'

As we neared the village, in his green livery jacket with crested silver buttons, Brown took back the reins and slackened the pace of the dog-cart going up Round Hill.

'Not that he thinks much of me. Or me of him either. Always on his beam ends by all accounts.'

'Well what if . . I mean, suppose . . what would you do . .? It's such a lovely house,' I had to finish lamely.

Brown took his time replying. We were well down the hill and picking up towards the houses.

Then 'Oh . .' he said

'. . go back big-game hunting, I reckon. They tell me there's tigers still in Cardigan, and one or two rhinos left in the Radnor Forest.'

My trouble was I asked too many questions.

On bringing up the subject of removing me to the country for a year, after I had previously been ill, at one time lingeringly so, my mother and father aided and abetted their decision by giving me the impression the peace and quiet – compared with moving house, say – would be as good as a seaside convalescence.

How little they knew about the country. There was hardly a restful moment. Every succeeding breath was crammed with activity and drama of one sort or another, with little room to languish.

In the greenest meadow the spider lay in wait for the blundered fly; along sylvan glades the hawk hunted fledgelings, a rustle in the hedgerow froze both mouse and shrew and in the sunniest of brooks jackpike scattered minnows like slivers of glass to smash-and-grab the silver roach. Rooks squabbled, starlings flocked and gossiped, small birds mobbed the robber jay and the interdependent lives of every species were conducted in a prevailing climate far less convalescent than fraught with daily happenings of crisis, predicament and outcome. Life teemed with life, making it, taking it, but teeming on and on nonetheless in endless commentary and constant errand.

The visible peace and quiet were merely an optical illusion, a random placing of earth, trees and sky put there by nature to mislead the casual passer-by.

Affairs of people and the goings-on in the village ran much the same course as those of wild society, producing their own quarrels, sensations and excitements to sustain the general pulse, and no sooner had the buzz of local interest in Uncle Will's windfall subsided than an event occurred which for chance discovery eclipsed the finding of the sovereigns and left it standing.

Just when I was thinking nothing much to write home about had happened lately. Just when Lammastide had come and gone leaving me in a period of personal doldrums, serving in the shop and becalmed among flotsams of mothballs and dolly-mixtures, pearl buttons and flypapers, catchpenny cures and remedies, candles, tin lanterns, bootlaces, dog biscuits and Rising Sun grate polish.

And feeling decidedly bored with it.

Even Lacey, the house-spider I had befriended in my room, whom I named after a glass-eyed gangling boy with eight arms and legs I knew at school, had a fit of the sulks and wouldn't come out of his crack in the woodwork. And all because one day I forgot his sugar-and-water, normally put out by the window.

I took to reading books – thre'penny paper novelettes – on my tea-time cheese, but if there was anything calculated to annoy me it was when I came across airy leapfrogging sentences like 'Winter became spring, and spring passed through summer into autumn before Felicity felt herself again', or 'Two long years were to go by before Clive returned to Staddlestones Hall'. Felicity couldn't have just sat about twiddling her thumbs, not for that amount of time, and something must have attracted Clive's attention to detain him so lengthily elsewhere.

At first I put it down to a writer's well run dry or field gone fallow, but now I saw there could be times in life when very little at all took place to occupy the interest.

I could recall only two things of note.

One Sunday afternoon there had been a thunderstorm of such symphonic proportions Auntie Fan came out from under the stairs, looked through a pelting window at swags of purple clouds disfiguring the sky like a boxer's bruises, said 'Sunday's thunder brings the death of learned men and judges!' and disappeared again into her cupboard to write a letter to the *Clanetty Clarion* on the situation in Europe since the seizure of the Rhineland.

Aunt Jessie's face was a picture.

'It's all that pobs and sugar,' she confided, back of hand. 'It softens up the cranium.'

But she was well and truly stumped when we read next morning of the sudden death of a leading legal figure, looking sideways at Auntie Fan for several days, weighing her up but keeping her conclusions to herself.

The other thing was, one evening Parry Gorick came

59

to the front door and asked if he could borrow my 'tater-hawk.

Uncle Wallace's lifelong friends and drinking companions, he and his partner Doubting Thomas, in business for themselves with a builders' yard across the green, were the classic comedy duo in real life. Doubting Thomas, sallow, set-faced and never been known to smile, replied 'Oh, I doubt it!' to almost any question and was the perfect foil for Parry's eccentric and outgoing disposition.

When they took on a job you could be certain they would swing round unexpectedly and clout innocent bystanders on the back of the neck with ladders, step into buckets of whitewash, burn bottoms accidentally with the blowlamp, nail each other's overalls to the door and run through all the slapstick routines and pantomime set-pieces as though they were the natural hazards of the job.

Personally I liked them. Unaware they might have made a fortune on the halls, at dinnertime they fried chops on a shovel like the navvies and would often ask you round the brazier if you happened to be passing. Which is why I fetched my 'tater-hawk at once and gave it over.

It was Aunt Jessie who said

'What do you want with a 'tater-hawk? You haven't got a garden.'

It all came out in an injured rush, from a man with strong religion and a fascinating hobby.

'Because I just spent God knows how long writing the Lord's Prayer on a grain of rice,' cried Parry. 'And what 'appened? The minute my back was turned, the bliddy canary hopped out of his cage and gobbled it up!'

'But why do you . .'

'. . want the hawk? To dance in front of his cage, and scare him witless!'

'Oh-h, Parry!'

Aunt Jessie stood him off with a look and made the most of her cadences.

60

'A big grown man, is it? You couldn't be so cruel.'

'Wait,' he said, 'you haven't heard the last of it. I was mending my boots on the table and my mouth was full of tacks. I opened it to shout at him and went and swallowed 'alf. Look well if I die of a rusty tummy, and none to shed a tear!'

How Aunt Jessie kept a straight face I don't know. But seeing him so sorry for himself she brought him in and gave him a dose of jalap off a spoon, soothing him with her gently lilting voice till he was more himself again and anxious to be grateful.

'Oh missis, you're an angel and a jewel,' he said. 'You know your doorbell's 'anging by a whisker? You been so good, I'll fix it if you like.'

'No thanks, Parry!'

Aunt Jessie spoke quickly, her mind's eye full of him rampant with a hammer.

'Er– p'raps you'd best be off now. That jollop won't take long to work.'

Parry nodded.

'By the way,' he mentioned. 'I saw the squire. He said tell Wallace not to go without seeing him, very partic'lar, when he delivers the groceries tomorrow.'

'I'll see he gets the message,' said Aunt Jessie.

Watching Parry down to the gate, under her breath she murmured, 'Poor old Parry. He couldn't glue the handle on a jerry.'

Then still half-thinking of the tacks she called out

'Mind how you sit down when you *do* go. You don't want to risk a puncture, not at your age!'

Uncle Wallace was not one of those servile, quiff-tipping shopkeepers, the more important and influential his customers the more he fawned and stretched his braces bowing them in and out. Anything but. A time-served master of his grocer's trade, he did not lightly let it be forgotten.

So it was nothing out of the ordinary to see an exchange of mutually respectful raised hats, sporty check cap and brown bowler, when we met the squire, rose in buttonhole and regimental-tied, on the steps of the Old Hall next day just before noon.

'G'morning, Wallace,' he barked. 'G'morning, my boy.'

Brisk and military-limbed, his shining face veined like a Christmas pomegranate, he adjusted his monocle and, as gentlemen do, awaited an introduction.

Uncle Wallace soon explained my presence.

'Capital!' said the squire. 'Couldn't be better. Just what we need, a bold young feller-me-lad!'

He hurried us indoors and we followed at a fast clip through a series of chilly rooms and passages, smelling of wet labrador and gun-oil, so lacking a woman's touch and spartan in their contrast to Miss Florence's beautiful flower-filled home. In the servants' hall he unlocked a heavy wooden door and conducted us down a narrow staircase to the warren of vaults below.

Only the squire and Briggs the butler were allowed in the wine cellars with their racks of bottles in pyramids and slumbering rows. It was their owner's declared intention to drink the lot before departing this life and anyone could see he had made a good start. More of the racks of unpainted pine were empty than full, for the squire, who might modestly have described himself as something of a connoisseur, was known in plainer terms as something of a tippler.

Incapability Brown, they hinted, was a baby at his mother's breast compared.

'What happened, d'y'see . .'

Talking as he led the way the squire took us to an adjoining room devoid of fittings but for an outsize kitchen dresser pulled into the centre of the floor.

Nailed to the bare brick wall behind him hung a decorators' dustsheet.

'. . makin' a bit more room the other day . . I manhandled the old dresser away from the wall, and lo and behold . .'

Giving the sheet a jerk the squire unveiled his discovery.

'. . a bricked-up doorway! Now what d'y'make of that?'

Not for nothing was I top of the class at mental arithmetic. Putting two and two together in a flash I stood well in the lee of Uncle Wallace.

'Is that what you meant . .?'

'Quite so, my boy,' exclaimed the squire. 'You shall be first through the hole!'

'We'll need tools,' said Uncle Wallace.

'Behind you in a bag,' said the squire.

'And it's going to take a while.'

'I've laid on lunch. Cold beef and pickles do?'

'And somebody ought to . .'

'. . let your dear wife know?'

The squire was quite bucked to have seen to every detail.

'I told Briggs if we weren't up in ten minutes to telephone and say you might be delayed an hour or two.'

Uncle Wallace looked resigned as he picked up hammer and chisel.

'My nosey-parker nature, it'll be my ruination. I just have to get to know.'

'Get to know what?' said the Reverend Powys, coming up behind us.

He claimed he had only dropped in to borrow a decent bottle of wine as the bishop was coming to dine that evening, but I had my doubts.

It could be the squire, a proven organiser, had asked

him to attend in case I needed a blessing going into the hole. Or the last rites coming out. I had a ballooning imagination and thoughts of Shropshire leg-eaters lurking in the shadows, fire-spitting toads and packs of fan-tailed rats as big as tabby-cats left my stomach jumping as Uncle Wallace set about loosening the first course of bricks.

Plus vividly remembered fireside winter's tales of Clipfoot Jack and Scraggie Aggie – the Shaley Clee bogles – liable to materialize anywhere dank and gloomy.

It was some time before a hole big enough for me to get through had been cut, but I helped myself unnoticed to a steadying glass of red wine with the cold roast beef and by then I was past caring.

'Now d'y'see why y'come in rather useful?' said the squire, lighting me a candle and tying one end of a ball of string to my ankle. 'We'd have been all day making a bigger hole.'

'Why the string?' I asked.

'In case you drop the candle!'

Against the Army mind I was only a novice; the squire had thought of everything.

Outward-bound it crossed my mind I might return a hero, with long-lost heirlooms in a box, or clutching ancient wills and parchments, the titles to earldoms, grants of land and unsuspected riches. But as it was, not long after, I crept back empty-handed – dusty, deflated and downcast – with never so much as a glimpse of fan-tailed rat or bogle.

'Well?' said the squire, as he gave me a hand back through the hole.

They stood round, brushing me down and breathing.

'Is there anything in there?'

'Only a lot of old wine racks,' I said. 'I didn't explore it all. The light was getting low.'

'Wine racks?' said the squire. 'Not um – er – full ones, by any chance?'

'Yes,' I said. 'Oh . .'

I reached back into the hole and pulled it through.

'. . I found this on one of them.'

'The cellar book,' said the squire, taking the leather-bound ledger from me. 'It's been mislaid for years.'

He frowned.

'But why would father . .?'

Slowly, as he riffled through the pages, Uncle Wallace and the Reverend Powys intent and bent on either side, confined by the low ceiling I felt the atmosphere draw suddenly close and become oppressive. Like woods and fields fall loud with silence at the onset of a storm.

Except this was neither ominous nor brooding. Only gathering in intensity as little lightnings of murmurs and remarks began to lick and flicker off the subterranean walls.

'Look here. The three chateaux . .'

'. . Lafite, Latour and Mouton-Rothschild . .'

'. . and look at the years . .'

'. . eighteen-ninety-six, 'ninety-nine and nineteen hundred!'

The discharges built rapidly into a crackle of excitement as they carried on.

'Fifty dozen of this, fifty of that . . .'

'. . and there's two whole pages of ports and old madeira.'

The squire mopped his sweating brow.

'And have y'seen the brandy? Hine, 'o-six, and Armagnac. A . . a hun– hundred dozen apiece?'

He sank back, overcome, his voice gone away to a whisper.

'I'll be drunk for ever,' he said, drunk at the prospect.

'*Sequitur patrem, non passibus aequis*,' intoned the Reverend Powys. ' "He follows his father with unequal steps"!'

'Virgil,' he sighed, and bowed to the inevitable.

That was the one held moment before I was suddenly

65

overtaken by the force of the storm erupting all around me. Then eyes staring and temples pounding, the squire sent me off at the double for paraffin lamps and a flashlight. By the time I returned they were going at the wall, in rolled-up sleeves and braces, like miners at a coal-face.

I stood alone, a would-be hero, left to my own devices as bricks and rubble rained down like the tumbling walls of Jericho.

They did not stop working till the doorway had been cleared and they could light the lamps and walk through unimpeded. The squire went in first with the flashlight, its strong blue-white beam revealing a length and breadth of cellarage I could not hope to have reported from the glow of a single candle.

'There's been an entire wing sealed off here, no less.'

And again he frowned.

'But why would father . .?'

And broke off.

'Unless it was to further his investment, and keep me from a toper's grave.'

It took an hour or more to check the racks and bins of grimy white-splashed bottles against the record in the book, inspecting curled and faded labels pinned to the wood and ticking off the entries as they tallied. Only now was I beginning to appreciate the extent of what I had lately been dismissing as not much of a find.

When Uncle Wallace read off the back of an envelope where he had been doing his sums I knew something of its enormity in total.

Maybe I was a hero after all.

'Well, squire, it must be nine or ten thousand bottles. Give or take a bottle or two.'

'Good Lord!' said a unison squire and Reverend Powys.

66

'And take a bottle or two we will,' enthused the squire. 'For this has been a day we'll long remember!'

Not that I did remember a great deal after that; not clearly. Only the inquisitive sun, as the afternoon wore on, hanging like an orb from the pelmet over the windows in the squire's locked study where, wreathed in beatific smiles and cobwebs, we held a wine-sipping fit for kings. More than that. Listening to informed opinion round me – for I was not excluded from any part of the ceremony – we ended with a bottle of port of better lineage than half the royal heads of Europe.

Finally, after three selected bottles of claret and one of a noble burgundy, all poured by the squire with consummate skill and panache, it was finishing the port that finished him.

With the aid of a befuddled Reverend Powys, dog-collar wilted to a rag, and later to suffer agonies of remorse having to explain himself to the dining bishop and his lady when he nodded off over the soup, Uncle Wallace and I guided the squire towards the drawing-room, the rekindled fires of incomparable vintage years burning like autumn beech trees in his cheeks.

Decanting him gently into a comfortable armchair, quiet as mice we tiptoed on our way.

We also had some explaining to do.

'What's the meaning of this?' said Aunt Jessie when we got home. 'Just look at the state you're in!'

'I had four glasses of wine and a port,' I babbled, bubble-lipped and cheeky. 'They didn't leave me out. They couldn't. I was first in through the hole and I'm a hero!'

'Hero?'

I jumped a mile as Aunt Jessie swung round to denounce me.

'You look more like a boiled owl to me!'

'Oh-h, Jessie love . .' swayed Uncle Wallace. '. . it's all my fault . .'

It was as far as he got.

For coming home three sheets in the wind, and having no sense of responsibility, she gave him a whack with a rattan carpet-beater she happened to have in her hand and chased us both upstairs, guarding our shins and giggling, to sleep it off.

Auntie Fan was disgusted.

Next morning, at breakfast, when the real explanations were over and done with – taking advantage of her forgiving nature, she said – Aunt Jessie uttered the words which were to change my life completely.

What I had been until then was of no importance; of what I wanted to be I had planned little and cared no more than that: regarding the present, just to be part and parcel made me passably content.

Until Aunt Jessie said

'I hear somebody's taken Michaelmas Cottage for the summer. A lady and her daughter.'

★   ★   ★

★ **6** ★

★

'Bet I know something you don't know!'

'What?'

'I haven't got anything on under this dressing-gown.'

I waited.

'Nothing at all. Not a stitch.'

Alert as a cornered cat, I waited.

'I took off all my clothes in the bedroom and I'm absolutely naked. I am. All over.'

By then she had laboured the point as far as was reasonably acceptable.

And still I watched. And waited.

'You don't believe me, do you?'

I shouldn't have said

'No!'

But I did.

'There then, see!'

In an impetuous flurry she tugged at her dressing-gown and threw it open. My adam's apple swelled to a goitre too burning-hot to swallow and I knew I would never doubt her word again.

She had no more on than a new-born babe.

'Well . . ?'

★ ★

Lacey was dead: to begin with. There was no doubt whatever about that. Like Old Marley, Lacey the spider was dead as a doornail.

It was going to be one of those days . .

I found him frail, dry and retracted, clutched in on himself like a miniature anemone corm, on the windowsill after breakfast one morning. I was truly sorry. Although we had not been on speaking terms lately I did the right thing by him and buried him in private ceremony under a loose floorboard in my room. In a Captain Webb matchbox. I felt he would have liked that, back in his natural habitat among the dusty joists.

. . definitely one of those days. I had that sinking feeling.

Further disruption came at dinnertime when we closed the shop from one till two. Left to mind themselves a minute the lamb chops burnt to a crisp, then the potatoes boiled dry and stuck to the bottom of the saucepan and the peas went hard as beads.

'Three out of three!' fumed Aunt Jessie. 'What can happen next?'

When she opened the oven door she found out. The queen pudding had abdicated.

'Oh-h,' she cried, pitching it out of the back door, dish and all, 'of all the contrary-minded . .! I'll kill myself, that's what I'll do. I'll take rat-poison, stab myself with a dagger, lie on the railway line and just as the train is coming, blow my brains out with a revolver!'

It needed a nice sit-down and a couple of cups of tea in quick succession before she simmered, 'Well, isn't it enough to make you?' and saw the funny side of it.

Then she sat back off the edge of her chair.

Just as I thought her temper was nicely subsiding the telephone rang.

'If that's for me, I'm out.'

'Suppose it's the police?'

'Oh, ta very much!'

Aunt Jessie drew forward again.

'Or the cottage hospital?' said Auntie Fan. 'Things happen in threes,' she went on. 'You said so yourself. The spider, the spoiled dinner . . there's sure to be something else. You wait and see.'

'It's Uncle Lloydwillie,' I said when I returned.

'There you are,' interrupted Auntie Fan. 'What did I tell you?'

Hastily she slapped together two slices of the bread-and-dripping we were making do with, grabbed her tea

71

with the other hand and made a beeline for her refuge under the stairs.

I tried to carry on as if nothing had happened.

'He wants to call by later on and take me to the Llandafty Music Festival. It's this weekend, starting Friday.'

Then I couldn't help but say

'What's the matter with Auntie Fan?'

Aunt Jessie bent down with a saucer of tea for Billingsgate, because it was good for him and made his fur shine.

'Well,' she said, beginning grandly, 'it's all a question of partition.'

'What?' I said, genuinely taken aback.

'Your Uncle Lloydwillie wants to build a Welsh Wall,' she explained. 'And Auntie Fan disagrees. Very strongly. Every time she sees him it's like a red rag to a bull.'

'Go on,' I said. 'You're pulling my leg.'

'In the seething cauldron of European politics, Auntie Fan says, seeing little states topple left, right and centre to armed aggression, there's an object lesson to be learned. United we stand, and so on. Now then, are you any the wiser?'

'No!'

'There's a good boy,' said a relieved Aunt Jessie, giving me one of her impulsive hugs. 'Neither am I!'

Sooner than expected, a few minutes before the shop opened for the afternoon, Uncle Lloydwillie arrived. The first thing he did when Aunt Jessie went to the door was present her with a yard of wire and the doorbell which had come off in his hand.

It had not affected his composure in the slightest.

'Good afternoon, Jessie.'

'Oh dear,' sighed Aunt Jessie. 'P'raps I should have

72

had Parry fix it after all, and risk him knocking the place down.'

'I trust I find you well?' said Uncle Lloydwillie, kissing her hand, making his entrance and striding over to sit down, all in a connected series of movements which demonstrated how splendidly he had the grand manner at his very beck and call.

As a professional musician, the look of him was half the battle. Even on an August day, tight-tailored and cut swanky, he wore a black overcoat with mole velvet lapels, purple bow-tie and celluloid collar, and carried an embossed cane and lavender gloves. Forswearing spats in high summer, his half-mast academic trousers revealed patent leather boots to complete the day's ensemble.

Posed there in the parlour he reminded me of one of those old sepia portraits of Toscanini; the same sensitive haunted oval face, the spare frame and straggling moustache; the same dark circles under black-dark smouldering eyes which sized you up, laid you bare in a moment, yet somehow begged your acceptance of a brooding inner passion too wrapped up with and too suffering of his art for any lasting peace of mind.

Women worshipped him, falling like ninepins at his feet, though he hardly ever noticed.

Able to improvise by the hour, a talent developed in his silent-cinema days, and sight-read and transpose like the platform gods of old, he gave lessons at home in piano, theory and harmony. Singing pupils, of whom he had an abundance of maiden ladies, he had to go round visiting. Auntie Prune had put her foot down there, convinced that amateur sopranos in full song were detrimental to the ornaments and rattled the dishes on the dresser.

Besides making the dog howl.

And Heaven knows, he was noisy enough. So much so, in a shaft of inspiration, Uncle Lloydwillie had aptly named him Offenbach.

Just now our visitor was cordially disposed.

Fine luminous hair the colour of November moon-beams fell over his ears and played like a restless St Elmo's fire round his forehead as he adjusted his gold nose-pinchers and got down to quizzing me right away.

'How's the piano-playing?'

'Coming along nicely, thanks,' I said.

'How about scales and exercises?'

'Oh . .'

I held back a little.

'No fibs, mind!'

'. . the same, after a fashion.'

'After a fashion? When I was your age,' he told me, 'you couldn't keep me away from the piano. Morning, noon and night.'

'Why did they make you practise so much?' I said.

'Nobody made me!' said Uncle Lloydwillie. 'Very often it's not the child who possesses the gift, it's the gift possesses the child.'

Lapping eloquent long-boned hands one on top of the other he let the remark sink in, then gave me a worldly wink that robbed it of any self-esteem or humbug.

After Aunt Jessie had packed me a bag, as we were leaving he went over to the cupboard under the stairs.

'And how's my fiery political opponent today?' he enquired, tapping her door with his cane. 'Come, come, I know you're in there.'

'Go and boil your head,' said Auntie Fan.

Uncle Lloydwillie did his best to sound hard done by.

'Well, good day to you, Myfanwy, just the same.'

'And make a mutton broth with it!' came the reply.

★   ★

Like quartern dough put by to prove, tiny town or overgrown village, whatever it was pleased to call itself, annually at festival-time Llandafty increased in size by

74

nearly twice the resident population, with rising excitement as the balm.

Its five pubs and a coaching inn booked out weeks before by leading lights and star performers, other competitors pitched tents and made encampment round the sheltered upland pasture where the festival took place, beneath the mountainous heights of Llandafty Hill.

When every plot was taken up, jabbering in half a dozen tongues, the rest descended on the community. There were Cossacks under the eaves, morris-men and maypole-girls in boxroom and attic, Bavarian bandsmen in the cellars, gauchos, gipsy fiddlers, exponents of balalaika and Welsh harp – come one, come all – under the sink, the settle, behind the mangle and curled up with the collie.

Anywhere at four-and-six a night where dimpled granny, respectable wife or widow could shove or shovel them in.

It was all hustle, bustle and go; late nights, tea-and-a-fag for breakfast, high jinks and low, sing-songs in the pub and the odd spot of bother. There were camp fires in the night, serenading men and soft-eyed women, verse-speakers and bards, duets, trios, quartets and complete male-voice choirs up from the pits and valleys; with Uncle Lloydwillie, chairman of the overworked, overwrought committee, brandishing his baton and list of entrants like a manic master of ceremonies in the middle of it.

And enjoying every minute.

His reliable little Austin Seven had made short work of the journey through the high clouds and higher hills of the westering marches and we reached Principality Place, his legacy bungalow on the hillside, in plenty of time for tea.

Not that we wanted much to eat. Half-way there we had stopped on Bob Major Clee, from whose summit you could count twenty-one church steeples, for the snack Auntie Prune had provided on the back seat.

The basket was like a lucky dip at the fair.

After the thermos leaking tepid tea I unpacked several hard-boiled eggs, one a duck's, a chunk of bread-pudding like a lead doorstop, another of cold spotted dick, a handful of monkey nuts and a few escaped aniseed balls.

Uncle Lloydwillie happened to catch my look.

'I know,' he said. 'I was thinking that myself.'

'Oh, I like everything,' I said, in quick amends. 'It's just . .'

'. . the combination,' he said for me.

Shelling the monkey nuts he mentioned

'Sunday evening's the big occasion, you know.'

He threw a nut at my head.

'Oh?' I said.

I saw it coming and dodged.

'I'll be doing Beethoven's piano concerto number three in D minor with the combined festival orchestra.'

'Who's the soloist?'

'I am!'

'Who's conducting?'

'Need you ask?'

'Then tell me about the Welsh Wall,' I said.

The question fetched him up abruptly.

In the pause I took a breath and said again

'Tell me all about the Welsh Wall.'

'It's my dream,' said Uncle Lloydwillie, a far-away look in his eye. 'To rival the Great Wall of China. Right along the line of Offa's Dyke.'

'Who's going to build it?'

'And it will be magnificent, I can tell you.'

'What will it cost?'

'The eighth wonder of the world.'

'Well who's going to man it?'

He came to, partly.

76

'Volunteers. Welsh volunteers.'

'And why? What's it all in aid of?'

Phrasing it so flippantly caused Uncle Lloydwillie to fix me with those black-dark smouldering eyes in that haunted oval face. Hunted almost, as if something was pursuing him from within.

'To keep the English out,' he said.

It might have been out of a deeply regarded national pride; for wanting to preserve the country of his abode in its wild untampered beauty, nourishing on its roots and tales and beloved Celtic legends; for a fervent desire to uphold the native speech and not to have to use the 'thin language' as he called it, from the other side of the border.

For any and all these reasons.

'What on earth for?' I asked him.

Yet they were by-the-by.

'Because they have no passion.'

He said.

We were still talking about that as we turned through the five-barred gate into his trim gravelled drive where I could see Auntie Prune and Meriel, their only daughter, coming out of doors to meet us.

Then logical argument was scattered to the winds.

The gravel lisped no louder than shingle as our feet touched it, but the moment they did an ambushing, flap-eared piratical dog with a black patch over one eye and too many teeth for taking chances hurtled out of the privet and straight at us. We leapt for dear life back into the car. Only just in time. As Uncle Lloydwillie slammed himself in, with a deafening crash Offenbach hit the door, exploding with barks like a demented jumping-jack.

Uncle Lloydwillie sat encased in his clothing.

'Call him off,' he spluttered through a wound-down crack in the window. 'Call him off, I tell you!'

Auntie Prune peered in at us.

'He's pleased to see you. He only wants to say hello, bless him.'

A vague, likeable, old-fashioned homebody in a blue cotton frock and pinny, she coaxed Offenbach away and quietened him down with a dinosaur bone.

Then we scuttled indoors.

'That damn dog. He gives me acid indigestion,' grumbled Uncle Lloydwillie.

'Never mind,' said Auntie Prune. 'There's fine weather for the festival. The *botel fach* says so.'

She indicated the 'little bottle', the home-made barometer kept on hers and many another kitchen sill. The water in the neck of the up-ended bulb-shaped bottle was high, a good sign, and Auntie Prune and all the neighbouring farming folk set great store by its forecast.

To me she suggested

'Why not go for a walk with our Meriel?'

And to her daughter

'Meri, take him down the meadow and show him all the preparations and the brand-new marquee.'

Then to Uncle Lloydwillie

'You ought to go and have a lie-down, love. From tomorrow you won't be off your feet.'

'All right,' we said, in chorus.

Somehow people could never go against Auntie Prune. Heart, hearth and hob of the home, she never raised her voice nor quarrelled with anybody.

Braided hair drawn back on the nape of her neck, her passive cheeks as smooth as the other side of a spoon, she cut the bread across her middle, told the bees when somebody was ailing and on cold and frosty mornings always gave her stays a warm in the oven before putting them on. Built not for speed but comfort, she went to church, lived her life, hoped to die and that was that.

With a husband so touched and volatile she had made a virtue of being in the background.

Meriel and I walked along in silence for quite some time. I had not seen her for going on two years and was never very good at picking up the threads. Slightly taller than me she was some months older, forward for her age and turning out pretty with her brunette hair and long dark lashes, taking very much after her mother's side. She walked differently now, I noticed; a young girl acquiring the assets of a young woman, donning them like new and longed-for clothes, anxious to be seen to her best advantage and make me aware of her too.

I trailed along, taking it all in, and didn't mind not speaking for a while. Something said previously had got me thinking.

After we had taken a look at this year's camp, like a tent-town in the Klondike, heard its similar din and admired the twin dragon pennants on the new central marquee, we strolled along a stony cart-track above the festival ground. Harvest teams on the broad expanse of Llandafty Hill, dusty men and sweating horses, were chest-deep amongst the first cut of the oat crop.

We sat down in the margin of a field like an empty room with only the carpet left, a shorn and even stubble, tinder-dry and crackling.

Meriel pushed up against me, warm-bodied and friendly.

'We haven't seen each other for ages.'

'No.'

'I used to like you then. Did you like me?'

'Well . . yes, I suppose so.'

My short answers would have to do. I was still thinking. I reached for an ear of oats to rub, on a pretext, but Meriel was pursuing me and would not allow me to put much space between us.

'Do you like me now? Do you think I take after our Mam?'

'Yes. Very much.'

'Dad says she's pretty as a picture.'

'She is,' I agreed.

'Am I . .' said Meriel artfully.

I rubbed the oat grains bare in the palm of my hand and crunched one or two, nutty and ripe, between my teeth.

'. . you know . . pretty?'

Husky, pollen on her breath gone to honey in her throat, her voice was the best thing about her. Taut and intimate as a yawn, it drew a curtain of privacy in the empty room and changed the carpet stubble to a close and downy quilt.

'I want to hear you tell me.'

All of a sudden it dawned on me.

'What did he mean, D minor?'

'Are you listening?' breathed Meriel.

'He doesn't make mistakes like that,' I said. 'Not Uncle Lloydwillie.'

'You mean C minor,' I said, as we sat down to supper. 'Beethoven's third piano concerto is in C minor.'

'Not now it isn't,' replied Uncle Lloydwillie. 'I rewrote it!'

Whatever else, you had to hand it to him for nerve.

Putting down his knife and fork he stretched behind him to one of the four pianos, always in easy reach, which had come with the bungalow willed to him by a retired music-loving lady some years before.

'Now pay attention . .'

He played the solo opening statement of the first movement in the original.

'. . and now tell me what you hear?'

He followed it with his version in the new key.

'It certainly sounds brighter,' I said.

'What else?'

'Well, firmer. More assertive.'

'Exactly!' beamed Uncle Lloydwillie. 'Because that's its proper key!'

He pulled a thoughtful face.

'You know, Beethoven couldn't have been himself just then, to miss a trick like that. If he slid down a rainbow now, poor fellow, and knocked upon the door, I'd have to put him straight.'

He turned back to the table and began to slice a sizzling toad-in-the-hole in portions and lift them onto plates.

'So all things considered, I re-copied the orchestra parts and composed my own cadenza.'

'It's sacrilege,' I said.

'Not a bit of it!' maintained Uncle Lloydwillie. 'An old revolutionary like Beethoven? He'll enjoy it . . once he gets used to it. And he ought to be pleased. I could have played the Grieg with less than half the bother.'

With nothing on his conscience he offered us the vegetables and handed round hot brown gravy before trying the toad-in-the-hole.

Smacking his lips he wheezed at his wife with a wicked leer

'Oh, there's tasty, love. *Real toad!*'

Auntie Prune shuddered and pushed her plate away. Meriel shrieked and dropped the gravy-jug. And when I hugged my sides, what with Beethoven sliding down the rainbow and stood corrected, devilish Uncle Lloydwillie and the bedlam of real gristly toad, she kicked me hard under the table.

'I ought to be mad at you, leaving me in the field like that. You almost ran away.'

'I had to go,' I said, 'and speak to Uncle Lloydwillie.'

'But I'm not now. I forgive you.'

Meriel was making the most of her voice again and I was alone in the bedroom with a naked wanton in a Welsh wool dressing-gown.

And on a Sunday evening too.

Half an hour earlier, playing and conducting from the keyboard to a packed marquee, Uncle Lloydwillie had given a spectacular performance of the Beethoven concerto. Most days he was hard to beat but on the evening that was his evening, and the climax to the festival, he rose to an occasion where it was fitting he should be unexcelled.

The audience gave him an ovation.

Flying hats and handbags, flowers and votive garlands filled the air. In transports of delight the music critic of the *Clanetty Clarion* tossed his trilby up and caught a better one coming down, and Uncle Lloydwillie couldn't have had a more devastating effect on his crowd of lady admirers had he laid about him with a leg of the grand piano.

Blocking the centre aisle, again they fell like skittles in an alley until he virtually had to step over them in a heap.

'Speech . . speech!' they cried.

'Oh no,' he said, declining. 'If I have an imperfection, it's my modesty.'

Picking her moment in the crush Meriel whispered to Auntie Prune she had a headache, and was it all right if we went on ahead and put the kettle on for when they got home? All the time I was in my room – fool enough to think she was lying down – she had been undressing and putting finishing touches to the plot she had been framing during a past three days which wore me to a shadow.

'Well . .?' she said again.

'Well what?'

With the same pout and impetuous flounce as she had opened her gown Meriel threw it off completely and bounced herself onto the bed.

'Please, Meri,' I implored her. 'Please get dressed. If ever they . .'

'They won't,' she cut me off. 'There's always a bit of a do for the committee after, and you know Dad, once he's in the limelight.'

Knowing it all along she lay back on the eiderdown in a submissive cartwheel.

'So come here to me,' she said, all dew and pollen-honey. 'I'll let you do something, if you ask me nicely.'

I had to go, but I was desperate.

Not only had I led a sheltered life but I had fixed views about becoming the plaything of designing older women, taller than me.

'You do like me, don't you?' said Meriel.

'I like you very much.'

'And I am pretty, aren't I?'

'Yes.'

'And attractive, and desirable?'

'Yes.'

'Well what are you waiting for?' she said.

Above all I would have given a king's ransom to be back in the shop, chatting to Aunt Jessie and dear old Auntie Fan, sharing jokes and jam tarts, safe and sound on my tea-time cheese.

Never again would I pick holes in those thre'penny novelettes.

There was a lot to be said for Cli—

I stopped dead in my thinking tracks.

That was it.

Saved at the last gasp: saved by Clive.
And Literature!

Flooding back to me, no, charging, like the cavalry to the rescue, came the turret-room scene. That time Clive had all but been seduced by the brazenly disrobing Corinna, scheming, by way of the convenient four-poster bed, to become mistress of Staddlestones Hall. Square-jawed and resourceful, had he not deftly turned the tables to save himself from a situation the replica of mine?

Considering it a literary gem at the time I had learned the passage off by heart. But would it – and memory – fail me now?

I pulled myself together . .

Clive looked down at the floor.

I looked down at the floor.

When he spoke it was earnestly, and from the heart.

Me no less; though mine was thumping loudly.

'Corinna,' he said.

'Meriel,' I said.

'What I have to say,' we continued, 'is best said now for both our sakes. It may be sacrifice on my part, but, knowing you as I do, respect outweighs such passions of the body as might possess me at this moment. I must be brave, I must be strong, to fight the urge which makes me want to take you in my arms and love you wildly, passionately, with every fibre of my being.'

Clive and I looked up now at Corinna and Meriel on the bed, where we saw them gazing spellbound at us. Our eyes were not a little troubled – it went on in the book – as we moved closer and took their hand in ours.

'But I know this cannot, must not, be. At least at present. One day, when time is ours for taking, and both of us need not resort to clandestine caresses, I shall come to you, as you will welcome me, Corinna, and then at last we'll know the meaning of a deep romantic love. Till then . .'

Clive sighed and said no more.

Nor did I. I couldn't. I was out of breath.

Meriel sat up on the bed. Her pretty chin was trembling.

'That . . that was the most beautiful thing I've ever had said to me in my life.'

I picked up her dressing-gown and helped her on with it, no longer the dewy fulsome temptress, so luring and alluring. Just Meriel in a daze, pink as a sugar mouse and no more wanton; pushy, adolescent, growing up and learning.

And also teaching me.

Just as she was leaving, brushing my cheek with a tearful kiss she said

'I'll never forget tonight. Never, as long as I live.'

'And I'll remember too,' I said, 'for every bit as long.'

'But why did you call me Corinna?'

★　　★　　★

★ 7 ★

★

'Where've they gone to?'

'Best not ask,' said Aunt Jessie.

'When are they coming back?'

'Oh, they'll be back . .'

'Will they be long?'

'. . leastways . . they've always come back before.'

Aunt Jessie seemed not to want to commit herself much at all.

'A few days,' she hedged, 'depending.'

'Depending on what?'

'Ask no questions,' said Aunt Jessie. 'At the beginning of September, every September, ask no questions and be told no lies. Would you like a drink of pop?'

'I wouldn't say no.'

'I'll go down and get you one.'

She left me hugging my knees on the box seat and looking out at my view over the valley.

Through constant shifts of light and shade created by still or scudding clouds in skies clear blue or changing, no two days nor even parts of days were the same.

What fashioned the wind I didn't know, but the wind sculpted the weather and the weather patterned the valley with its in-facing galleries of hills so that the land – being also The Land – though ever the same, was never quite the same.

Something else was different too. Something about me. Not just superficially, about the eyes that took a note of outside changes, but whatever was responsible for changes going on within. Like a cutting in a pot, like the scented geraniums, clove and peppermint, beside me on the windowsill, I felt I had begun to strike root and it was time for growing up.

Check and dormancy were over. I was suddenly astir.

87

Llandafty and Meriel had been good for me.

Not knowing how it came about, only that it did, I had been mindful of a recent strengthening in my middle region, somewhere round my belt-buckle, a girding-up and self-reliance where once I might have hung fire, shy of making moves and not sure how to handle both myself and situations.

Trying it out resisting Meriel had been first step, lesson and experiment in one.

Part of me was all for taking up her offer, but she had been too bold, too there, too ready for the asking. That, and my fixed views about being cornered into compliance, had been decisive in keeping me back.

When the real time came, in not just an alignment of bodies for purpose' sake and nothing deeper, I wanted some truer source of consonance with the girl, whoever she may be. Some other bond more durable on which to base the physical first-meeting.

Helping myself to what was laid out on a platter, like a greedy guest at a wedding, formed no part of my scheme of things.

One thing about those thre'penny novels. They were hot on high ideals.

Still, it was all over now . .

'Why did you?'

'Why did I what?'

'Call me Corinna?' she persisted.

. . although I had so nearly come a cropper.

At school I was the quickest liar in our class. Not the biggest. Given time, Tom Snow and Billy Newbold were better in nucleus and invention, but I was rated higher for my promptness of response.

'It's Greek,' I said, and never turned a hair. 'It means "little girl". It's always been my special name for you.'

Meriel went out walking on air, but I couldn't feel

safe until I heard her bedroom door close and knew she must be putting on her nightie.

Beguiling Uncle Wiley was supposedly the one never stuck for an answer; a portly bowfront gentleman who kept the antique shop in Clett, in a tight corner he had the manoeuvrability of a ratchet screwdriver.

The bit of him in me perhaps was nothing to be proud of, but it sometimes came in handy.

Thinking about this and that, watching the harvesting in full swing and the new lie of the land standing out in sharper focus as clattering close-cut fields began to give the lights and shades so much more room to play in, I hadn't stirred from my seat at the window when Aunt Jessie came back with some of her gassy ginger pop, humming strong with yeast.

She looked across my shoulder.

'Nice to see everywhere getting a short-back-and-sides,' she said, 'sprucing up for autumn. Did you enjoy yourself at Uncle Lloydwillie's?'

'Yes,' I said, sipping my pop. 'What's been happening while I was away?'

'Well, I finally got the letter from your mother asking if you could come and stay.'

'It took a long time getting here, didn't it?'

'Not really,' said Aunt Jessie. 'Auntie Fan was using it to wedge a cupboard. She forgot to give it me in June when it arrived.'

'Anything else?'

'The school inspector's been round.'

'And?'

'Rebuilding won't be finished in time, so you don't go back until the middle of October.'

'What?!' I yelled, grabbing Aunt Jessie in a boisterous hug and squeeze.

'There, I knew that would cheer you up,' she said. 'Did you like Principality Place? It's a nice bungalow, isn't it?'

'You'll never guess,' I said.

I laughed because the thought of it still tickled me.

'They've got an indoor lavatory. *And* it's got a lid!'

But at the very mention Aunt Jessie's face took on the look of longing Uncle Lloydwillie's had assumed when I asked him about the Welsh Wall.

'It's my dream,' she echoed. 'Some day . . a proper toilet, snug and warm, in the corner by the downstairs back.'

'Well, you never know,' I said.

'Never come no-time for me,' sighed Aunt Jessie.

Of her two most frequent sayings, that was one of them.

As she turned to go, offhand I said

'Oh, er – by the way, Aunt Jessie. Those long trousers of mine. Would it be all right if I started wearing them every day?'

'Well I never!' she said. 'Before that happened I thought I'd see a square moon rise . '

That was the other one.

'. . in an oblong sky!'

At a time where lately I was having to revise some of my opinions in the light of the increasing strides of youth I was also having second thoughts about one or two of my uncles. Up to now Uncle Will had led the field unchallenged as diverse and interesting in character but now I saw Uncle Lloydwillie had claim to run him close.

The Llandafty weekend had left me with two outstanding recollections.

One, happening on top of the Bob Major Clee after

lunch and just before we drove away, though it nearly frightened me out of my wits, remained as only scalp-tingling. The Great Tone was a fact. It was there. The second was quite mad. Shot with lunacy and beyond the scope of ordinary thinking.

In other words only to be expected of a man like Uncle Lloydwillie.

The morning after the festival I was up with the lark, sitting in the garden waiting for Uncle Wallace to come and call for me as arranged. From my seat on the sunny sloping lawn, down in the distance I could see the tent-town dismantling. To roustabout shouts floating faintly over the hill, pennants fluttering like flags on a howdah, the big marquee was beginning to sink to the ground as ponderous and slowly as a lowering elephant. Gathering up their own tents in the night a number of competitors and performers had already stolen silently away and the Cossacks were saddling up for the long trot back to Russia.

Which way back to Moscow, Mrs Jones-ski?
First left at the traffic lights. You can't miss it, boyoh!
Und vhich vay to Bavaria?
Same again, and turn right at Mrs Llewellyn's!
Ach, so.
Off they went, the foreigners, as, fags lit and hands in pockets, the gauchos slouched off back to Cardiff.

Good-natured Auntie Prune came out with a souvenir programme for me, signed by all the principals. She would always go to endless trouble like that. Wishing me goodbye she took my picture with a box-brownie and gave me a kiss, instructions how to make a *botel fach* for some reason, a little pot of mind-your-own-business for no reason, and another leaden sample from her inexhaustible bread-pudding mine.

91

There must have been a seam of it, somewhere up the mountain.

I thanked her as best I could, even though when I stood up it pulled my arm down like a bell-clapper.

Catching sight of Meriel down by the rockery I made towards her, listing heavily.

'What's wrong with you?' she said.

'Nothing,' I panted. 'I was all right till I picked this bread-pudding up!'

'Don't let Mam hear you say that.'

Half-hidden by cushions of thrift and late-blooming alpines I placed it where it wouldn't notice – in among the other rocks – and we walked on together.

'You didn't mind, did you,' said Meriel, 'about last night?'

At first she sounded apologetic.

'I thought afterwards . . I mean, I wouldn't want you to think . .'

Contrite almost.

'I never thought anything of the sort,' I said.

'Then you will come back again?'

'I will, I promise.'

'You already have.'

'What?'

'Promised,' said Meriel, artful as ever and voicing it low. ' "One day, when time is ours for taking, I shall come to you . ." That's what you said.'

Her flicked glance hit the middles of my eyes like a thrown dart.

'I'll hold you to that promise. And just remember. Every saint has his past and every sinner his future!'

Steeped in husky honey, blushing red and thankful we were still in sight of the bungalow, I might have been compromised even then but for the timely intervention of Uncle Lloydwillie.

'Stop! Stop, I say!'

92

We looked round startled as he bore down on us full tilt across the dip of the lawn.

'Stop whatever you're doing and come and help me.'

It was clear he needed me urgently back at the house. Strange to relate, everyone else had vanished. Auntie Prune was nowhere around, Offenbach conspicuous by his absence, and seeing her father fasten onto me Meriel took it as her cue and fled.

As if they all knew.

'What a day for the books. What a day for the books, I tell you!'

Had recognised the signs and knew he was on another rampage.

'Come on. Make haste. There's not a moment to lose!'

At the terrace his full-throated shout tore the fragile air of morning, urging me on directly, and once inside his study, from corner cupboard, shelf and cubby-hole, he started to pull out a lifetime's collection of books – of every size and subject – and pile them into my arms.

Staggering under a load of his own he hurried me back to the lawn to dot them down on their spines with fan-spread open leaves.

It took no end of journeys before some few hundred were spaced out, regular as bedding plants, all over the mowered grass. And still not satisfied Uncle Lloydwillie would not rest – nor let me – till all his music books and scores were out and airing too.

Only then, a shepherd amid his flock, did he look at me and say

'There now, can't you feel it? The sun? Those magnetic rays of sunrise, drawing you up to Heaven?'

I could, but 'What's that got to do with the books?' I said. 'Are they damp or something?'

Uncle Lloydwillie shook his head over me, as though I should have known better.

'Books,' he lectured me, 'left on their own and never

read, they're nothing more than prisoners . . the shelves their cells, the libraries their prisons. To think of all that scholarship, locked up mute and wasting.'

'But we can get them out if we want to,' I said, 'can't we?'

'It's not enough,' said Uncle Lloydwillie. 'That's why once a year I set them free and flying, the great works of the greatest minds . . poems, plays and novels, the lives of saints and soldiers, heroic tales and histories, philosophy and music. Up they go to Heaven in the updraught of the sun and drop again to earth in the downpour of the gentle rain . . all the truth, the beauty and the knowledge, dispersed in sprinkling raindrops to refresh the soul of man.'

Funded by an inexpressible fount of joy and good-will . .

'I like to think it does a bit of good . . somehow . . somewhere.'

. . he lifted up impassioned arms and threw his head back to the cloudless azure sky.

Bright dancing sunlight enhanced the winter moonbeams of his hair, turning them golden in a halo.

And his face was the face of an angel.

I cried and laughed alternately all the way home.

Crying for Uncle Lloydwillie, for his talent, for his bonnet full of beautiful balmy bees, and because he was touched and mad, touching and mad, and mad again, divinely.

Laughing because my eyes had been drawn back briefly to the rockery where black-patched Offenbach, having found and pirated my abandoned bread-pudding, was lying stiffer than a board, legs up, looking seedy.

The more I thought the more I cried and laughed. And cried and laughed and laughed and cried again.

Aunt Jessie said it was my age. Boys go through it just the same, and I was overtired as well.

How could I tell her any different?

Before the week was out, under cloak of dusk and just as Aunt Jessie was busy shutting up shop – bolting the door, dropping the holland blinds and setting the nightly fleet of mousetraps, one of which always caught Auntie Fan dipping in the sugar sack – Uncle Wallace slipped home quietly from his mysterious expedition.

Now I was able to find out more about it; the reason why, no sooner had he brought me back from Llandafty, he had rolled half a dozen empty five-gallon barrels into the back of his van, picked up Uncle Ben and departed in a southerly direction.

I guessed their destination was a seaport but was hard put to discover which. It could have been Swansea, Bristol, Plymouth or Portsmouth even. Wherever it was, now ashore and nightwatchman at a bonded warehouse, Uncle Ben had an old shipmate whom they had gone to visit to lay in a stock of spirits, rum mostly, and a gallon or two of brandy, at nod-and-a-wink prices.

Assurances that everything was straight and above-board, that such things did exist as cask evaporation, topping-up allowance and natural waste and spillage pursuant to the trade left Aunt Jessie unimpressed.

'Natural spillage my foot. Helped on with a bang from a bung-hammer more likely!'

She remained convinced they were the next best thing to a couple of rum-runners, and the less she knew about it, or told me, the better.

Well aware that life was rarely what it seemed and always a shrewd judge of character, dosing me with brimstone-and-treacle after my peculiar bout of laughing and crying, she had said 'That young Meriel hasn't been leading you a dance, has she?'

'Aunt Jessie!'

I gave a guilty start.

'There's a real little barrowload of monkeys,' she said. 'Always panting for a chap. Lick the spoon.'

'Oh, she's not so bad. Ugh-h . .!'

'Then why have you gone redder than Clett fire-engine?'

'It's the brimstone.'

'Come again?'

I didn't believe it myself the second time I said it.

The following morning I helped haul the barrels down the cellar.

Like Stir-up Sunday – the twenty-fifth after Trinity – for making Christmas puddings, time is allotted in country living for most pursuits but Uncle Wallace needed no command nor collect to name the day for starting on his pumpkin rum and brandy.

The pumpkins told him when.

'They ripen to a turn,' he said, 'and go the colour of a Leicester cheese.'

Testing as we went we walked along a row of orange pumpkins, grouped on the settle and bellied like a mayor and corporation, though more exotic in array, the turbaned caliphs of an eastern court. Rapped with an enquiring knuckle each gave back a satisfactory resonance.

'Sound and sweet as Dawley bells,' pronounced Uncle Wallace.

If he said so it was so, for he put everybody in the shade when it came to growing pumpkins. Every one a specimen, not one less than thirty pounds, the largest a goliath more than fifty, it was as much as the pair of us could do to grip it round the girth and carry to a bench to get to work on.

I watched closely as the ritual began, made easy by the practised hand of years.

Using a sharp-pointed knife Uncle Wallace cut a hexagonal lid from the top of the shell, leaving the dried stalk for a handle. Then he scooped out fibrous tissue and the seeds till he had a perfect hollow globe of rich ripe pumpkin flesh. From inside arose the fruitiest of odours and rivulets of amber juice were seeping down as sweet as oils of glycerine.

We took it back to the settle and while I ran off a jug of new navy rum Uncle Wallace tipped a pound of demerara in the pumpkin. Then he let me pour the rum on, cane-light and astringent, to just above half-way.

Now what?' I said.

'Nothing,' said Uncle Wallace, 'but let the rum draw out the juices.'

He made a small vent-hole, fitted it with a straw, then replaced the lid, dribbling a lit candle along the join to seal and give it a craftsman's finish.

'The hard part is the waiting, till we tap it in December.'

Making the pumpkin rum was the last working task I undertook in any sensible frame of mind, apart from when Aunt Jessie sent me down to Michaelmas Cottage the next day with a pound of fresh-ground coffee.

'A lady ordered it on the telephone,' she said. 'From down south by her accent, and very lah-di-dah. She seemed surprised we had our own machine for grinding.'

'Oh, didn't you know?' growled Uncle Wallace, surly for him. 'A five-bob trip from London and we're all a lot of savages. Cannibals, p'raps, in Wales.'

And to me he said

'When you get there tell her we hardly ever drink rainwater out of stumps . .'

'You'll do no such thing,' said Aunt Jessie.

'. . nor use a kipper for a bookmark!'

'I wasn't going to,' I said.

'It seems to me somebody put too much rum in last night's cocoa,' observed Aunt Jessie. 'Unless it was too little cocoa in his rum.'

'It was only a drop left over,' he said, flexing his jaw ruefully. 'Oh dear, I've got the megrims. My face feels like a busdriver's behind.'

'Serve you right too!'

'How about the brimstone-and-treacle, Aunt Jessie?' I suggested. 'It's just the stuff . .'

For a man with a hangover he moved fast. I barely got out of the kitchen.

And then . .

There I was, arrived at Michaelmas Cottage. Me, Jack-the-lad, smart as paint, plenty of lip, full of myself and life, enjoying it; brown as a berry, lark-heeled and whistling, free as air and beholden to none.

I vaulted the garden gate and rang the doorbell with my elbow, seeing how far I could push my luck.

. . the door opened . .

I looked at her. She looked at me.

. . and the world turned under my feet.

It was the moment when I put away my toys.

★   ★   ★

★ 8 ★

★

Just in the meeting of our eyes everything came right for both of us. There was nothing said. Nothing needed to be said. I knew it. She knew it. That instantly attracted to one another, and wholly compatible, we were not two as one, but closer; and joined the better that the words remained unspoken.

Once met, as there could be no thought of parting, nor could there be of any going back. From now on we would go along together, hand-in-hand, into a future lit with constancy and promise, that idyllic landscape, over the hills and far away, ringed by a bridle rainbow and iridescent as an image caught and carried in a bubble.

The one seen in the once when we are young and destiny is lenient with daydream.

In only a moment, one which saw the loss of all my selfishness, I pledged her all I had to give – myself – and she made over all she had to me. It was the strangest feeling. As though some precious renewal, a nodding recognition from a time before was taking place.

Because of it, straightway we were old friends re-united, the boy and girl next door, sweethearts growing up, true valentines become adoring lovers; then the happy couple, newly-weds in a cottage with roses round the door, silver-wedding parents and golden-wedding grand-parents – though we never aged a bit – Darby and Joan before Jack and Jill had learned each other's names.

Racing ahead I knew my heart's desire, and witnessed it so clearly.

It was hours before I got back to the shop. Aunt Jessie and Auntie Fan were about to sit down to tea without me.

'Don't say you've been down Michaelmas Cottage all this time?' they said. 'It isn't possible.'

'It is, and I've got a lot to tell you.'

'Fancy that,' said Aunt Jessie. 'Have a cup of tea.'

'Yes, fancy that,' repeated Auntie Fan. 'Have a piece of treacle tart.'

I scanned one face and then the other.

'Billingsgate put his foot in it,' said Aunt Jessie.

'And we can't sell treacle tart with paw marks,' said Auntie Fan. 'It isn't good for business.'

Neither one was giving much away.

Then overdoing manners as they drank their tea, and nibbling at their treacle tart genteelly,

'I wonder if he's going to tell us about Laylie?' began Aunt Jessie. 'And how well she's doing at the ballet school in Surrey?'

'Or her father, in the army in India?' said Auntie Fan. 'He's coming home next year, you know.'

'Oh, won't that be exciting?'

'Though I expect Laylie's mother will continue her cookery column and the articles she writes for ladies' magazines,' said Aunt Jessie. 'She must be very clever.'

Seeing my mouth drop open, Auntie Fan was first to weaken, dissolving in a spray of treacly crumbs and giggles. Then Aunt Jessie's face was slipping and she gurgled in her tea at my disbelieving look that they could know so much.

'Listen,' I said, 'a joke's a joke . .'

It was for them. They slapped their knees and wobbled on their cheeses.

'. . but how could you . .?'

'A little bird told us,' said Aunt Jessie. 'And by the way, Laylie's short for Laelia.'

'We had to look that up,' said Auntie Fan. 'She was a wood-nymph in mythog– mythogol– mytholog– oh, drat these blessed teeth!'

Which set them off again, and this time it was catching.

'That's better,' grinned Aunt Jessie, when I had to

laugh. 'As a matter of fact it was Briggs, the squire's butler, stopping by to get some matches.'

'Well how would *he* know?'

'Because the squire owns Michaelmas Cottage and lets it out occasionally,' answered Aunt Jessie.

'Because Laylie's father is an officer in the squire's old regiment . .' went on Auntie Fan.

'. . and because . . oh, that's enough of explanations!' said Aunt Jessie.

'Anyhow,' she said.

When we had a moment to ourselves, checking round the shelves, after the shop was shut and it was quiet enough to begin the monthly stocktaking.

Auntie Fan was in the back preparing supper.

'I'm glad you've found a nice companion.'

'Oh yes?' I said. 'We're nearly out of Brasso.'

'No, really. We can manage in the shop and it will be a change to have a friend to go about with. You're always on your own.'

'I don't mind that,' I said. 'I never have.'

'Go on,' said Aunt Jessie. 'You know you're very taken.'

'I am,' I admitted. 'Did you know, both our birthdays are the first week in October? And we're exactly the same age and height.'

'Is that important?'

'To me it is. When Meriel . .'

'Yes?'

I slowed up.

'Oh, nothing. We're also out of Zebo.'

'Some people!' said Aunt Jessie, sounding vexed.

'And there's not a lot of soapflakes. What?'

'Could try the patience of a saint, let alone a Polly Pry. And what took you so long at Michaelmas Cottage?'

'Laylie asked me in,' I said. 'I watched her do her

practice in the garden. Her mother gave us sandwiches and coffee, then Laylie danced again and I played the piano. When it was time to come home her mother said "Maind hew yew gew crorssing the rewd"!'

'She said what?' said Auntie Fan, coming in. 'Supper's ready.'

I repeated what I'd said.

'Was she sucking half a lemon?'

'Not that I noticed.'

'And they got the cheek to think *we* got a accent!' said Auntie Fan.

Looking back I put it down to something to do with Uncle Ben's pet theory of Time.

It had to be.

Never a one to sleep the clock round, throughout the lamp-lit hours he read in reams and pondered gravely, often on and into moonset, about life's deeper issues. From a while ago when he had come to oil and regulate Aunt Jessie's mantel chimer, just lately gone contrary, I recalled a conversation.

'Now what would you reckon to the notion Time stands still, young shaver, and it's us who pass on through it?'

'It makes no sense,' I said. 'The clock hands move, and night must follow day.'

A dab hand with a timepiece, turnip watch to parlour ticker, Uncle Ben dipped his bantam feather in the linseed and sighed to be so weighty.

'Part of creation's riddle and mortal man's illusion. Did he but know, Time only passes – so to speak – according to his means of spending it.'

'You'll have to explain that,' I said. 'I'm no good at conundrums.'

'It's very simple. You take five minutes. If a starving

103

man had only that to eat his fill, or you were sparking with your best girl in the haystack . .'

The clock struck once, behaving itself again, as Uncle Ben tickled it contented.

'. . those five minutes would be over in a wink. But say I sat you on that hot stove there, five excruciating minutes? Oh, would that seem like an age?'

'Well, yes . .' I said, '. . but . .'

'The selfsame period of time,' pointed out Uncle Ben, to all intents made motionless. And short or long by man's own passage through it. You'll find, as many a one before you, a joyous heart and time has wings. Make life an uphill struggle and you sip eternity by the spoonful.'

Rum idea or reasoned argument – Time brought to heel and stationed by Experience – it was one I couldn't counter, not just then.

In any case, put to the test, some of the truth was not long in emerging.

Alone together, together by ourselves, that was all the company we needed. Without delay and feeling duty-bound to share it, I acquainted Laylie with The Land – able to unfold it in all respects as native now, as My Land – and far and wide we made our pathways through it.

We began by looking round us close to home, meeting characters Laylie thought the people of a fiction.

'You're making them up,' she said. 'I don't believe a word of it.'

'Then come and see them for yourself,' I challenged.

The village cast obligingly paraded.

On her regular journey round the churchyard little Grannie Higgs bustled by with Cledwyn purring in the carrier bag.

'Rain or shine he has his constitutional,' she said. 'I let him ride because he's getting on, and not so game now, for a moggie.'

And her a widow twice and rising eighty-three.

Then Mr Daddy Rhys was squinting through tin spectacles, past his holly nose and piling drifts of whiskers.

'I had to bring him in again. He got the gripes, old Dobbin.'

With nowhere – so they said – to sit indoors,

'Don't blame me,' said Mrs Maudie Garbett, as fixed as ever in the garden. 'You picked the windfalls up yourself and fed him.'

Wrapped in a shawl and the old man's woollen comforter a down-at-heel moke with knotted mane and ribs like railings stared from the front-room window, breathing draughty as a flue and looking anything but fit for labour.

'We've always shared the fireside, him and me,' said Daddy Rhys. 'If he should die and go Up Yonder, I'll sell my 'ouse and go in lodgings.'

'Oh, there's heartbreak,' sympathised Mrs Maudie Garbett. Only to add, 'Can I have first refusal on your chairs?'

I looked enquiringly at Laylie.

'All right,' she said, conceding.

Another day we stopped to watch Little Humphries – the youngest of three nameless Humphries brothers, Little, Middle and Big – being wound up and down the wellshaft in a bucket as the country cure for whooping-cough. Then on we went by invitation to the builders', for sausages on a griddle and mugs of tea so strong a mouse could trot on it. True to form Doubting Thomas backed a barrow into the brazier, upset the kettle and blew Parry's pork-pie hat off in a cloud of steam and phrases.

Going back the way we came, attracted by commotions round the well-top, we found that Little Humphries had turned fractious. Got out at the bottom, sucking his thumb and perched on the iron bucket-rail some sixty feet below, he was refusing to come up. Safe from the strap, ignoring dangled sweets and deaf to promises, nothing they could do would make him budge.

He said he liked it there, among the ferns and water.

'Try the bogles,' I said to Middle and Big. 'They always used to scare me into nightmares.'

It didn't take a minute.

At breakneck speed his brothers wound up Little Humphries, wailing skywards in the bucket and feared that Clipfoot Jack – one foot and a hoof – and Scraggie Aggie, a-clutching through the water, would have him for their supper.

Again I looked at Laylie.

'All right,' she said, 'all right! But I still say nobody could have so many uncles.'

At the harvest festival, bright-cheeked and country-suited, knocking bonnets, stubbing toes and begging pardon, barricading pews and bursting hassocks, they almost packed the church out.

Mid cornucopias of flowers, of fruit and given produce, sheaves of barley, decorative bread and ropes of onions, pears in melting mounds and apples red as embers, with collar wings awry and spotted throttlers, they bellowed out the grand old harvest hymns and set the rafters ringing.

Uncle Lloydwillie came specially to play the organ, Handel Daniels led the anthem, and the eight remaining Ready Boys of the Wrekin – plus sundry other uncles like Uncle Joss and Uncle Reuben – took on tenor, bass and baritone and fought the choir to a standstill. Proudly beside their men, made slips of girls again, my aunts glanced coy and sidelong, showed their love and sat up close to hear the sermon.

The best of all the harvest hymns to close with, a hurried spill of silver in the plate, then having ploughed the vocal fields my uncles scattered. Down to the Lamb and Flag to lay the dust and wet their whistles.

Horizon to horizon they had Sunday-come and gone, trampling the ground and thundering, like a great stampede of buffalo across the western plains.

I couldn't look at Laylie's face a third time. It must have been a study.

After that, setting our sights on far Tibet and Samarkand, we went in search of wild and lonely places, the ones I'd gazed so long at from the attic window.

Sufficient to ourselves, inseparable and kindred, we wended, roved and wandered where the valley wind blew silvery as carters' bells, attractive to the ear and tingling. Trailing excited laughter like coloured tails and streamers, sometimes we were high-flown kites, making the most of bracing currents, gliding and buffeting over the delft-blue distant land. At other times we floated side by side in silence and slow motion, lazy boy and girl balloons withdrawn among the clouds in quiet communion.

Sent through the mystic force that mother earth inspired in her children there were days of an inexplicable flinging madness when we leapt for joy in sheer abandonment receiving it. Breathless we raced to the very tops of hills, stretched our arms and launched away on reckless pinions, dropping down slopes and rocky hillsides, young eagles from the eyrie, calling loud and shrill, fiercely paired and never to be caged nor captured.

Playing foxcubs, we had dens in brambly covers. Secret forms concealed our lain-down bodies, like silken hares in purple upland patches. Undressing fast and never shy we dived and swam naked in deep cold-rushing streams, then fell to dry on sunny banks, kissing and embracing among dipper and kingfisher, goldfinches in their prides and darting dragonflies.

Touching and trembling – never quite sure if it was from being on the brink or from the ice-cold water – by

mutual consent we time and time again stopped short
with neither one prepared to make the running.

As the last, and first for us, expression, completeness
was eluding us, contingent on a time – not yet – and on
some other place.

On the shared date of our birthday, in our green-
roofed timber house built up in a woodland oak tree, we
sat cross-legged and had a party.

Blowing out the candles on the cake,

'What did you wish?' said Laylie.

'That we could go on being as we are, that's all.'

'We've only got another week, you know.'

'A week at most,' I said. 'I don't know where the time
went. Has it flown, or were we flying through it?'

'You'll have to explain that,' said Laylie.

'That's just what *I* said. It's all to do with Uncle Ben,
and starving men, and sparking with my best girl in a
haystack!'

'What's sparking?'

'Making love,' I said.

'We haven't gone as far as that,' said Laylie.

'No, I know. Not really.'

'Is it because . .' we both said.

'. . you don't want to?' said Laylie.

'. . or you don't want me to?' I said.

Once again, that mutual act of pausing.

But when our eyes met, like that first time at Michaelmas Cottage, they met in reassurance, reminded of a
wordless bond and confluence of spirit we cherished from
the outset.

The tree-house was our place reserved for talking,
where often we would go to make our plans or settle
arguments. From it we could see the brackened wildwood,
its rides, its footworn paths and glades of dappled sunlight.

In a breeze they call a kissing-wind about the house, just light enough to play along the eaves and tug the casement latches, red and gold and stoked up in the fires of autumn, leaves from the Joseph-coated trees were hurrying from the branches, knowing there were only so many dropping days to Christmas. As numerous as snow-fall they whirled around and made no sound descending.

Up into the tree-house there rose a penetrating quiet, the hush of leaf-fall, and with it came an air of rest and of anticipation.

The days were growing short and it was time to put some questions.

'I've been wanting to ask you . .' began Laylie.

'Ask me what?'

'It's difficult.'

'Well try.'

'Those times we almost did . .'

'When we might have done and didn't?' I said.

'You never made the slightest move to . . to touch me. In that invasive way.'

'Invasive? That's a good one!'

'How else can I describe it?'

'It sounds so posh and boarding-school.'

'Oh, do shut up and listen. I'm serious. In a . . a taking, possessive way, I mean. Not all the time you've known me.'

'There's time and place for everything,' I said, 'and when it's right we'll each know, for the other. It ought to be like that to be remembered. Taking or possessing don't come into it for me.'

'That other girl . .'

'Who, Meriel?'

'Was it really like you told me?'

'Every bit,' I said. 'Recited party-piece and all.'

'But why?'

'Why what?'

'Why didn't you, when you could have, and so easily?'

Unable to prevent myself I moved closer to Laylie and took her hand in mine.

Square-jawed and resourceful, I said

'Because I was brave, and strong, and being noble. Just like this minute. Fighting the urge to take you in my arms and love you, wildly, passionately, Meri– er – Laylie, er – Corinna!'

Exasperated Laylie pulled her hand away and biffed me.

'Tck-oh! How do they put up with you at home?'

I laughed and said, 'They love me!'

In a spiralling swirl of leaves amid the Joseph-coated splendour, in an intimate, fallen, all-pervading autumn stillness, high up in the woodland tree-house,

'So do I.'

Said Laylie.

★　　★　　★

★ **9** ★

★

With Aunt Jessie and Auntie Fan sound asleep in bed and Uncle Wallace and his Saturday boon companions in the tap-room of the Lamb and Flag, at ten o'clock at night I slipped quietly out of the back door and by darksome lane and shadows of the hedges made my way to Michaelmas Cottage.

It was Laylie's last night in the village. She was leaving with her mother in the morning, and had asked me down so we could say goodbye.

'Can you get out all right,' she said, 'and back again?'

'Of course,' I said. 'But why so late?'

'I daresay we'll be packing until after nine at least. And late at night is always best for parting.'

The rooms downstairs were unoccupied and curtain-drawn as I went in through the cottage gate, with only a lamp-glow from an upper window.

Finding the door left on the latch I opened it and called out

'Laylie?'

She came onto the landing and partly down the stairs to meet me.

'Why is it so dark down here?' I said.

'I had something to attend to in the bedroom. I forgot to leave a light on.'

'Where's your mother?'

'She had to go to London with the luggage, there's so much of it. She's driving back to pick me up tomorrow.'

'But you said . .'

'What did I say?'

'That you'd be busy. Till nine o'clock or after.'

'Well things have changed a little,' said Laylie, 'but come and see what I've been doing.'

I followed her towards the lamp-lit bedroom.

It was then I smelt a rare perfume of roses.

Her sudden kiss took me by surprise just at the

doorway, its fullness and its difference from the kisses by the water.

'In the tree-house you never asked me what *I* wished for on my birthday.'

'What did you wish?' I said.

'To have an opportunity,' said Laylie. 'And when the chance occurred I chose a time, and made a place, for both of us.'

In the early evening when their scent was at its strongest, catching the last resplendent late-flush of the blowing summer roses, she had gathered a basketful of petals – deepest cream and damask pink and crimson – and spread them, a coverlet of fragrance, inches deep across the bed. Long strands of autumn-blazing red Virginia creeper were woven round the curving bedrails, poetic as a bower, and turning the old brass ornamental bedstead to a filigree of gold beneath the low-hung ceiling, glowing yellow lamplight brought out with subtle warmth the mingling musk, the spice and sweetness of the plundered roses.

In a breath like that which holds so still between the sea-tides, from the ebbing of the summer till the coming in of autumn, cradled in the lap of time as on an endless billow, we kissed and drew together.

Mainsprings might unwind at times like tempered snails, at others fizzing round like catherine-wheels, I didn't know the how and why of it. I only knew there comes a moment in Experience when It and Time stand still beyond imagining, in perfect love and union.

We lay unclothed and drank of all its beauty.

Choose neither women nor linen by lamplight, there ran the country saying.

How sere was its counsel.

Her dancer's body trained for expression even in repose, Laylie was modelled exquisitely in every line.

Graceful disciplines had shaped her slender limbs and figure to classical proportion, making a reality the wood-nymph of a legend, Laelia, lithe and supple in her bower.

So surely did it lie within her province, if she had said let's run away – over the hills and far away to the wild and lonely places, to manna moss and crystal springs – for ever, I would have chosen her by any light and left without a backward glance.

'Those times . .' she said again.

'. . we almost did . .' I prompted gently.

'. . and yet we didn't. Maybe I didn't want to, not enough, just then,' said Laylie. 'I couldn't find a reason.'

'Well something held us back,' I said.

'I'm glad it did. I know now what it was for me. It had to be a special place, the one we would remember. And this is where I want to, now, before we part.'

Infused with love and drenched in all our senses from the rush of rose perfume our act released from crushing petals, we sought, of two, to make a sanctuary of one.

Just once, in the beginning, though I felt no sense of conquest nor invasion, Laylie cried out and called my name; and in a little while, just once, as it was over, she pulled her body taut and fell away from me. In my own tranquillity I lay against her side, drifting through my skin like gauze and into hers as tired in our fulfilment, pulling our petalled coverlet around us, we closed our eyes and slept.

I awoke refreshed at early dawn to the sound of the oil-lamp puttering, making a soft plop-plop in the still love-heavy room.

Laylie stirred, but only for a moment, as I crept out from beside her, hating to leave the rose-strewn bower where she would wake to find me gone. Knowing I must not linger, in sentiment or self, I quickly dressed, then bent to print a last kiss on her brow for a remembrance.

With no one yet about to see I returned head down along dejected lanes, kicking at stones and chilled to the bone by a clinging vaporous mist, the cold shawls of a mid-October morning. Safe again in my attic bedroom I wrestled out of my mist-damp clothes and wondered . . was it all in dreaming?

Till from my pocket fell a petal from a blood-red autumn rose.

★   ★   ★

★ **10** ★

★

With the coming of Hallowe'en, to keep the witches out, at dusk Aunt Jessie rapped the doorstep and all the downstairs windows with a bible, we stayed close to the glead of our evening fireside and before going to bed, so not to break the custom, left an empty dish and jug of salty water on the table. Now if any witch or sprite should venture down the chimney there would be neither bit nor bite to feed them.

It was a time of ancient frights, of old beliefs, and scares and superstitions. If you must come home at dead of night, then don't look over your shoulder.

On the Saturday before Armistice Sunday a frosty pall of fog came rolling down the hills to muffle up the windows thick as felt and greyer than a sheep-fleece. As we were sitting down to breakfast, much too soon for unexpected callers, the back-door knocker went off like a gunshot. Billingsgate took to his paws and ran for cover, Aunt Jessie almost jumped out of her slippers and Auntie Fan dropped her glasses in the marmalade.

Even my own heart skipped a beat and made me swallow.

Slowly the door squeezed open just an inch.

With what relief a whimsical voice came piping round the door-jamb.

'It's only me, missis. Only Jones.'

'Oh-h, Only,' gasped Aunt Jessie, glad to see a friend in bogle weather. 'I nearly had the staggers. Come indoors and shut the fog out.'

Thin as a wisp and well past seventy a little weazen man in clothes of days gone by stepped out of another century and straight into the kitchen.

'I hope I'm not intruding?'

'Don't be daft. You know you're always welcome.'

He stood his tiplight in the corner, heaved a bulky pedlar's pack off his back and sat down next to me.

Blowing on mittened hands he said

117

'I wouldn't mind a drop of tea, my sonny.'

I poured him out a cup.

'How are you keeping, Only?'

'Oh, rough and ready, missis, like the ratcatcher's dog.'

'What have you had for breakfast?'

'A rasher of fog and a fried snowball!'

'I thought as much,' said Aunt Jessie, laying a heaped-up plate in front of him.

'Missis,' said Only Jones, 'you're a veritable godsend.' He picked up knife and fork. 'Where some there are who wouldn't give a Eskimo a coughdrop.'

Last of the travelling packmen, no farm nor cottage too remote to call on, for fifty years he had tramped the border hills and valleys, setting out wares in every parlour from his portable haberdashery and bringing the pleasure of a visitor to many an isolated farmer's wife and family starved of market news and hearsay.

He read fortunes in the cup for wistful maids and wide-eyed servant girls, carried their lovesick notes to swains on other farms, sold everything useful under the sun – almanacs to lampwicks, curling tongs to garters, penny whistles to babies' bibs and pacifiers – and was valued near and far as a practitioner of herbal healing.

At country fairs and in village streets he was forever being waylaid by bent old men with gravel or the grave-yard cough, butter-fat wives with palpitations and, regularly, pale young girls in fixes.

To serve them all he stood by three prescriptions: Doctor Purdy's Poultice for everything external; for everything internal, Stott and Hickey's Mixture, said to warm the bosom of a corpse or start a tractor in a blizzard; while for young girls with old stories it was two penn'orth of Ladies' Sure Reliever, a recipe of his own concoction in a discreet blue tincture bottle.

In next to no time he had polished off a hearty

118

breakfast, mopping up with relish the bacon dip and vinegar. He would not sit back to take his ease. With travelling in his blood and walking the mainstay of his living, seeing the fog was lifting seemed to spur him into being on the move again.

To pay his way in kind he rummaged out and gave Aunt Jessie a fancy bottle of smelling salts and some pomade for Uncle Wallace. Auntie Fan received a wishbone brooch when she bought herself a bottle of the cure-all mixture for her wintery complaints.

'Stott and Hickey,' she read off the label. 'They call it Hot and Sticky, but it always does the trick.'

'And now for you, my sonny . .'

Putting on his pack and eyeing me a minute Only Jones took my tea-cup, swished the dregs and up-ended it in the saucer.

Studying the leaves he rhymed

'Two distant hearts I see, and truly plighted as the fates decree. Where you are you will not stay, but come again another day.' And then, in afterthought, 'Good news very shortly. The answer to a question, in a letter. And a sum of money coming, for a member of the household.'

For some reason Auntie Fan's glasses slipped and nearly went in the marmalade again.

'Only Jones,' said Aunt Jessie, who had known him from a little girl, 'if there's a smoother-tongued old rascal on this planet . .!'

The moment he tipped his hat and was out of the house, departing into the fog as suddenly as he arrived, I was staring at the tea-leaves for myself, though there was nothing I could decipher in their pattern.

Auntie Fan looked dry as a stick at me.

'Message-in-the-teacup!' she scoffed. 'Don't tell me you believe all that jiggery-pokery?'

'As if I would,' I answered.

'I thought you had better sense.'

119

'I have,' I insisted.

But when the postman called I rushed to get the letters.

Convinced she must have won a cash prize in the Titbits competition, Auntie Fan beat me to the doormat by a short head.

Up in my room, on the box seat by the window, I settled down to read my letters, two from Laylie and the weekly one sent by my mother. Though it contained my usual pocket-money postal order I was half-afraid to open it. Despite what Only Jones had said, it might be giving me answer in the negative to the important question I had raised a week or more ago. Then it occurred to me, if he was right about the distant hearts and truly plighted, the news inside could well be to my liking.

Taking a breath I opened the envelope and hurried through its contents. My hopes were dashed immediately. There was no outright refusal, but no mention at all of what I so badly wanted to know, keeping me on tenter-hooks, was even worse for me.

To add to that, written a couple of days apart and caught up with each other in the post, both of Laylie's letters seemed low and in the depths of woe. After the holidays, when she had done only her basic ballet exercises in the mornings, returning to school she was having to put in some very hard work indeed. The hours of class and strict routine were taking their toll and page after page of troubles came pouring out in her neat artistic handwriting.

Going back to school, and a different one at that, had undermined me too. Even losing a year through illness I was still streets ahead of the other pupils. An assiduous student of the classroom ceiling, I was put into the leavers' form – Standard X7 – while my new headmaster con-sidered what to do with me.

Fed up with irksome days, the thoroughly depressing weather, and beset with problems from news I'd had and hadn't had, cupping my chin in my hands I fell into a gloomy reverie as I looked out over Evensong brook and all along the valley to The Land.

Today it gave no consolation.

Clearing the uplands the fog had come bundling down to lower ground but the transient lights and shades, so essential to the passing picture, had all gone into hiding. On a cartridge-paper sky, sketched in unreflecting charcoal, the familiar triple line of hills — delft-blue, delphinium and purple – was changed to uniformly grey, and then to mourning black, a layered smudge like sooty smoke along the skyline.

Life was crowding in on me. Its odds were all against me.

As much affected by Laylie's absence as she was obviously missing me, I plunged deeper and deeper into a wallowing bout of self-pity. Common sense all drained away, and with it will to rally. Where spiteful forces wait to pounce on just such a luckless wanderer, I somehow left the safety of myself and passed into an abstract, a mental void and darkness gripping as a tomb.

How long I sat there, five or fifty minutes . .

As soon as the gentle hands were placed upon my shoulders, for the first time in direct contact, in their touch and without a trace of apprehension I recognised my attendant guiding spirit. Never to be thought of as a ghost, more a presence in the night, whoever had been watching over me from my beginning occupancy of the small room up among the slates and stars, she had drawn near – I was sure it was a lady – in her concern for my well-being.

It does not do to be astray in astral places.

My distress had summoned her swiftly to her charge from planes beyond a veil, and like the laying-on of hands

121

for sickness, I felt at once an ease of heartache and a comforting.

Not until I was restored into myself again, relieved of all my burden, did the hands relax their care of me. Better still, they had bestowed a longer-lasting benefit. In my heart of hearts, where we so seldom go, I knew now spiritually I would never be deserted.

And when I looked the ring of hills was blue and bright once more. The fickle lights and shades were out to play again, the pleasure of the passing scene a part of me.

Overcome with gratitude, 'Lady,' I tried to say, 'dear lady, if you can hear me . .'

But as I spoke her presence took alarm and went from me. In the room I heard the brush of watered silk along the wainscoting, perceiving too a scent of mignonette that wasn't there before.

Half in a trance, my letters in a scatter on the floor, I was still sitting silently when Aunt Jessie happened to look in on me.

'Oh, I'm sorry,' she said. 'Is it an awkward moment? Have you had upsetting news?'

'No, no, it isn't that, Aunt Jessie . .'

I started off with hesitation.

'. . but she was here. In broad daylight, in this very room.'

'Who was, love?'

Then it all came blurting out.

'The lady. She was wonderful. I wasn't a bit frightened. The one who . . it's when she . . when I'm . .'

'Now steady on, and don't get so excited.'

'But you don't understand.'

Aunt Jessie lifted up a finger.

'Understand?'

She came and sat beside me at the window.

'What don't I understand,' she said, 'with all the room so full of mignonette?'

And while we looked together at the meandering brook, the valley in the fog and the distant backcloth of the brightened hills, for the first time like one adult to another, she began to talk to and confide in me. She told me of her early married days to Uncle Wallace, about setting up in business and their high hopes for the family they so much wanted. Then how two miscarriages in succession had left her distraught and much too likely to be ill again to risk another pregnancy.

Gradually, although she spent many a day and sleepless night sitting where I so often sat, contemplating the emptiness, the years as stretching infinite as The Land, and the daily gnawing sadness of a childless marriage, she picked up the pieces of her life again.

But she had never been quite, and hopelessly, alone.

Always, in her blackest moments, the spirit lady had come to keep her company, laying on unseen hands and giving Aunt Jessie the courage to face another day and faith enough to know that she too, no matter what, would never be deserted.

'So you see,' said Aunt Jessie, 'I've had my share of tribulations, in your room, with your view from the window, and aided by your lady. There's times I would have broken my heart, I think, if I hadn't had a place to rest and let her come to me.'

'But do you know who it is?' I said.

'No,' said Aunt Jessie. 'Only that she's here.'

'Does anyone else know?'

'No, I never told a soul. It was my secret, and now it's mine and yours.'

'Maybe that's best,' I said, 'and how she best prefers it.'

Aunt Jessie sighed.

'Maybe it is. She's been a blessing to me though, especially when it's in my nature to get in a stew over every little thing .. whether this, whether that, whether

123

I'll ever get a holiday by the sea.' She pursed her lips. 'Or even a proper lavvy, come to think of it.'

The indoor toilet, as a topic of conversation, was almost a fixation with Aunt Jessie.

The times I'd heard her going on.

'That one down the bottom of the garden? Pff . .! Where's the sense calling it a convenience if it damn'well isn't? That's what *I* say!'

'Well, you never know,' I said.

I seemed to remember saying that before.

'Never come no-time for me,' said Aunt Jessie.

And hearing that before.

'Anyway, I'm glad we had a little chat.'

'So am I, Aunt Jessie.'

'It's cheered me up no end.'

'Me too.'

Taken into her grown-up confidence I smiled as she ruffled my hair and gave me a bigger-than-usual hug.

'Getting yourself in a state,' she said reprovingly. 'Things always turn out right, you know.'

Then, standing up,

'They have to! Now, is there anything else you want to know before I go?'

'How did Only Jones get his name?'

'From his catch-phrase, everywhere he goes. "It's only me, missis. Only Jones"!'

'And what's eye-money?'

'When the old folks die round here they always have two coins put on their eyes to keep them shut when they're laid out.'

'That's done it,' I said. 'I gave Laylie one of my half-sovereigns as a token.'

'Oh, there's no problem,' said Aunt Jessie. 'They'll just have to bury you with one eye open!'

'And lastly . .' I said.

'Yes?'

124

'What *is* Everything Taken Away, like Mrs Lily Prospero had?'

'Why, what did you think it was?' said Aunt Jessie.

I told her. Buns and pies and bits of cake dropping down the awful stitched-up cavity with thud or splash, depending on what had gone before.

Aunt Jessie went off downstairs, stumbling on the rails and shaking every tread with laughter.

'Oh dear . . herkle-herkle . . that's priceless. You'll be the death of me, you will, straight! Wait till I tell our Fan . . herkle-herkle. Still, as long as I die laughing . . herkle-her-kle . . I reckon it's as good a way to go as any other!'

Five minutes later she was back again.

'My brains will never save my feet,' she said. 'I clean forgot what I came upstairs to tell you. Only Jones was right. I got a letter from your mother too. She says yes, you can stay with us for Christmas if you like.'

I got into bed that night full of admiration for the intuitive Only Jones. It was blowing a gale outside. As the old house grumbled in the pushing wind I pictured the untiring packman plodding his pitch-dark ways through the worst of winter, when underfoot was like a midden, carrying his tiplight, the old-fashioned turnpike-man's lightstick with a lantern on one end and a little burning brazier on the other.

Bedding children seeing it twinkle across the hilltops would swear they had seen a shooting star or comet, or perhaps the flickering candles of the night-walking Long-mossen Folk, the vanished race of mountain inhabitants from the Long Mynd.

Too tired to keep track of the tiplight's will-o'-the-wisp progress I yawned as lazy as a dormouse, turned on my side and snuggled down with knees drawn up and paws across my stomach.

★   ★

Armistice Sunday came and passed with my uncles making a brave show at church, wearing blue suits with black armbands and jingling their rows of Great War medals. They laid a wreath of poppies on Uncle Mogg's grave and after that gathered down the lower end of the churchyard in an unexplained huddle. I wondered why they were so engrossed in conversation and why, when I walked towards them, they sauntered away whistling and looking at the sky.

All I heard Uncle Dick the corporal say was

'That's agreed then. Now leave the rest to me.'

It was probably some old compaigners' business; with influence in high places, notoriety in low, they were always scheming schemes or up to something.

Apart from that, November was unremarkable except that my voice was definitely breaking.

And with no mistake.

No longer able to pretend I had a cold in the head I had to resign myself never to hitting top C again, or even G. Lately I had been lucky to make the C below that, and that was becoming a liability. But at least the transition was taking place smoothly and not leaving me with a raucous halfway-house of a voice like somebody yodelling down a drainpipe.

I had a suspicion too of fuzzy whiskers on my cheeks, but Uncle Wallace said I didn't need to shave them, not just yet. Put a bit of butter on, he teased, and let the cat lick 'em off!

After the recent bad patch, ever since the visit of my guardian lady, things began to go well. Laylie's letters were happier, as were mine to her, and I seemed better able to withstand the drag of days at school. Even Percy Pugh, at variance with the house since June, had begun to deliver the milk again. Furthermore, Auntie Fan won five pounds in the *Clett Journal* bonny baby contest, another of Only

Jones's predictions coming true. So all in all the traditional black month, the one of slaughter, was turning out a not-unpleasant time.

In it I rejoiced particularly to see the demise of two of my arch-enemies, Mr Morris and Nottingham John.

All my life I hated pigs.

To look down from my room on to two vacated sties in neighbouring gardens gave me a tremendous satisfaction. At the crack of dawn one morning the executioner butcher had set up bench and gibbet, and Mr Morris, the pinkest and most well-nourished of porkers, and swilling Nottingham John, snouting wet in his neat-cuffed trotters, became gutted carcases and piles of offal, of no more consequence to me.

To every pig his Martinmas, and it does surely come.

One dinnertime at the beginning of December Uncle Wallace was perturbed by a telephone call he received from Aberystwyth. Elderly Aunt Martha had been taken very poorly and wanted her favourite niece – Aunt Jessie – to go to her at once. It looked quite serious, Uncle Herbert said. Come prepared to stay the week.

They were relatives I did not know, on Aunt Jessie's side.

'Look after her for a week?' she flared up. 'The old nuisance. Doesn't she know it's Christmas in the shop? Well I won't go!'

'Oh, there's uncharitable,' said Uncle Wallace.

'Listen to me. Our Martha's been knocking at death's door so often, if they opened it and let her in she'd drop down dead at the novelty!'

'It's up to you then, Jessie. I won't try to persuade you. But she did promise you her Worcester dinner-service when she's finally laid to rest.'

'Hmmph, when!' huffed Aunt Jessie, very put out. 'I tell you, if I do go it'll be only under sufferance.'

But thinking it over, agree to go she did.

A week later to the day I met the half-past five bus at the end of the road because Uncle Wallace had asked me to, as also the week before he had asked me to go with her to the station and see her safely on the Aberystwyth connection.

Aunt Jessie could watch any train or bus go out without realizing she should be on it.

'Hello,' I said. 'Here, let me take your suitcase, Aunt Jessie. Isn't it dark? Did you have a nice week? Was the weather all right?'

'Yes, no and no,' said Aunt Jessie. 'It was a bit of a wasted journey, if you ask me.'

'How do you mean?'

'I mean it was a false alarm again. Believe me, I'll have earned that Worcester service by the time I get it. Aunt Martha was no more ill than she ever is, and it's very peculiar . .'

'What?'

'. . when I said well then, I might as well go back midweek, she had a terrible relapse. A really nasty turn.'

'No?' I said. 'I wonder why that was?'

'Histrionics,' sniffed Aunt Jessie. 'Pure histrionics!'

It had taken us only a few minutes to walk back down Church Road to the shop.

'How's everything at home?' said Aunt Jessie.

'The shop burned down,' I told her. 'Uncle Wallace got the mumps and Auntie Fan ran off with the postman.'

'Ha-ha, very funny!'

'Otherwise, the same as usual.'

The lights were on in the windows but neither Uncle Wallace nor Auntie Fan were behind the counter.

'What's happened to our Fan?'

'Perhaps she's in the back,' I said.

'In that case, where's Wallace?'

'Perhaps he's in the back as well.'

'Tck, it's the same as usual all right!'

On the warpath, peeling off her gloves and fuming after a tiring journey, never mind the unattended shop, Aunt Jessie marched through to the kitchen – still no-one around – and then threw open the door of the back kitchen.

There they all were . .

'Oh-h . .!'

. . the reception committee; Auntie Fan, all the Ready Boys of the Wrekin, got up neat and tidy, Uncle Wallace in his Sunday suit, his hair brilliantined and bum-parted – straight down the middle – and carrying his bowler hat.

At the sight of them Aunt Jessie gave an indrawn breath and fell back on her heels as I came in and closed the door behind her.

They looked as solemn as a jury.

'What's going on?' she said.

Going up like a skyrocket and bursting at the height of her conclusions she cried

'Somebody's dead, that's it. I knew it!'

'Nobody's dead, Jessie,' said Uncle Wallace.

'Dying then?'

'Nobody's dying neither.'

'Billingsgate's been run over,' gasped Aunt Jessie, getting more extravagant and flustered.

'Oh-h, poor Billy!'

'No, he's all right,' said Uncle Wallace, 'the last I saw of him.'

'Well what is it then?' Aunt Jessie exploded at him. 'Stood there holding your bowler hat like you're round the blinking cenotaph!'

Looking round wildly, in the far corner her eye caught a change of colour in the kitchen.

'And who on earth's done *that*?'

The back-larder door had been painted a glossy polar white and a round holly garland with red ribbon and a bunch of sparkling festive bells hung in the middle panel.

Uncle Wallace stepped forward and gave her a new brass key.

'Go on,' he said. 'Open up.'

Subdued a little now, knowing something was definitely afoot, Aunt Jessie took the key, turned the lock and pushed open the door.

'Happy Christmas, Jessie,' said Uncle Wallace quietly.

Sworn to secrecy and promoted shop manager during the hectic pre-Christmas period while Uncle Wallace was busy with the rest of my uncles, kept apart and purposely not poking my nose, now I saw revealed the fruits of all their labours.

Living on the premises, supervised by Uncle Dick the corporal and cooked for like a regiment by Auntie Fan, all the while Aunt Jessie was away the Ready Boys had worked from first light through till dark converting the back-larder – never full of anything except sacks and bits of lumber – into a gleaming white-tiled flush toilet of the latest design. Including all the proper fitments, even to a lid. Digging, brickwork and connecting up the plumbing, using their wealth of practical talent, had all been taken care of by my first-class team of uncles.

Looking past Aunt Jessie's back I could also see a little hand-basin, complete with towel and soap, chintz curtains at the frosted window, and a vase of chrysanthemums pretty on the windowsill.

Nothing, no nicety of detail, had been omitted.

'There's even a magazine rack, Jessie, and a new enamel stove to keep the place warm,' said Uncle Wallace. 'Now you'll never have to go down the garden to pay a visit again. And does it go a treat?' he added proudly.

Like launching a liner in a shipyard, ceremonially he demonstrated by pulling the chain. As the sound of the powerful waterfall flush died away, with a send-off cheer

'Happy Christmas,' we all joined in.

It was the very best of moments.

A bundle of mixed emotions, Aunt Jessie had just stood throughout, fast-rooted to the spot. I saw her shoulders quivering, suddenly too small to bear the load of being held so dearly, and when she turned to face her husband her eyes were beautiful as bluebells.

'You . . you big soft ha'porth,' she said.

'Yes love,' he said.

'Going to all that trouble . .'

'Yes love,' he said.

'. . and all that expense.'

'Yes love,' he said.

'And stop saying "Yes love", will you, like a great big polly-parrot? You . . you . .'

'There there, Jessie,' he said, consoling her in his arms while she wept and wept for love of him.

Not that he was any paragon of virtue, but in all their years together she hadn't had much to take him to task over, except he would leave his boots in a jumble in the fender, one coming and one going.

Still wearing his gaffer's hat and judging the moment, efficient corporal Uncle Dick said

'Well, that seems to be that then. A good job, boys, well and truly done. Now we'll be off down the Lamb for a celebration pint.'

He ushered out his squad and I followed with Auntie Fan, leaving Aunt Jessie still hugging onto Uncle Wallace – all six feet and twenty stone of him – as if he might rise up and disappear into thin air like the angel he was, taking her toilet fit for a queen with him into Paradise.

Every year, like every story, should have a happy ending.

And that is how it came to be Christmas.

★

'You mean to say it was a put-up job?' said Aunt Jessie next day. 'Our Martha was in on it all the time?'

'She had to be,' confessed Uncle Wallace. 'How else could I get you from under our feet?'

'And I went and fell for it,' said Aunt Jessie. 'Talk about a ninny!'

'Never mind,' said Uncle Wallace. 'You got what you'd set your heart on, didn't you?'

'Oh, you can use it too,' said Aunt Jessie generously. 'Use it and welcome.'

'Not me,' he declared. 'I'll stick with the glory-hole down the garden. I can't leave the male-voice choir stranded. We're rehearsing for the carol concert.'

And Christmas truly was all around; there was a snap in the air like a pulled cracker. Plain as a pikestaff, plain as the nose on your frost-nipped face, it was Christmas everywhere.

It showed in a general increase in mirth and merriment, in children's best behaviour, in overstuffed pillar-boxes and fuller shops, in the jollier expressions of people passing, the breath on some of them like a hot mince pie, and in the lamps that bade you look in at their cosy evening windows.

There was a vicarage social and bun-struggle, the candle-lit service of nine lessons and carols, and a tanner hop – the Mistletoe Ball – in the village hall where clodhopping youths in pungent suits and snow-white scarves, hair slicked down with tapaline, shed mothballs like mint imperials and did the foxtrot with carthorse girls in singed satin dresses and shoes the size of gravy-boats. Till fumes from the coughing-hot coke stove drove them away from faded paper-chains and withered bough, away from Dolly Teece, piano, and Mr Treadwell, drums and vocal requests, round the back in the shivery night for a bit of slap-and-tickle.

And when Uncle Reuben called, as he annually did –

to Make the Arrangements – I knew it was really getting on for Christmas.

The grandest figure of a man, he farmed for himself, yeoman-fashion, high up on Pitchley Edge.

From tethering boots, hewn across the shoulders like the bossbeam of a barn, he rose up as a genie leaves bottle, widening as he went.

Frosts had flayed and the stubble sun inflamed his face until it assumed a ruddy hue to go with all the weathers, while in its midst there grew a shelf-like large moustache – ornate and waxed and fine – on which his nose took pride of place as quite the best ornament in the house.

If he had a fault, his temper, like some apples, was not a good keeper.

Three Aunt Alices could have walked in his shadow instead of the one I saw, half a pace behind him on the step. Quiet as an autumn cobweb, as estimably spun and pearled, she always dressed in grey set off with mauve or violet. Undemonstrative and shy, you had to get to know her; and whenever you saw her, nodding to every little breeze, she passed on her serenity and brought your better side out, like a pressed flower in a book.

She simply doted on an old-maid cat called Madge who slept in her sewing basket and had paws as delicate as bridal slippers.

I just sat and listened as over tea with a spot of something in it – seeing it was Christmas – they talked.

'Pretty much as we always do then,' began Uncle Reuben. 'Bring Jessie . . oh, and the boy this time . . Bachelor Billy and our Teddie's wife up to the farm . .'

'Righto,' said Uncle Wallace.

'. . Teddie will see to the children . .'

Uncle Wallace gave a nod.

'. . and Wiley, Joss and Belle will go from Clett directly to Miss Addie's. That leaves . .'

'Bert and Amy, Dick and Millie, Tom and Vinnie, Fred and Tilly . .' reeled off Uncle Wallace.

'. . to get to my place one way or another, then on we go from there. Oh er –'

'No, I won't forget,' said Uncle Wallace. 'I never do.'

He poured a parting tot of whisky into Uncle Reuben's tea and I could see why he called year after year to make mostly the same arrangements. It was well-known that since Madge had once got miaowing-drunk on rum sauce from the Christmas pudding Aunt Alice wouldn't keep even a medicinal drop in the house.

Who began the custom nobody could quite recall, but for years past, like the gathering of the clans, the family had taken to assembling in their numbers for a real old-time Christmas at great-grandmother Adelaide's farm-house.

So commandingly high and resembling an ancient stone fortress atop Pitchley Edge, looking down on Uncle Reuben's farm in the distance it seemed you could cover it with the palm of your outstretched hand. Then in her eighties, the last time I had seen great-grandmother Adelaide, whom everybody called Miss Addie, thinking it was Queen Victoria in lace cap and black taffeta, I remembered bowing from the waist like a pageboy.

Because she didn't travel well – the same as good wine, she said – Auntie Fan always went with Billingsgate, along with Parry Gorick and Doubting Thomas, to have Christmas dinner with great-granny Woodspring and Uncle Will and Uncle Ben. Every year Parry and Thomas offered to do the washing-up and every year, quick as light, everybody said oh no, no . . they mustn't even think of it.

There was only one other small matter to attend to, one beyond the organizing capacity of Uncle Reuben I would have thought, but

'Don't worry, boy,' he said, taking the question off the tip of my tongue. 'It's almost bound to snow.'

'How do you . .?'

'Don't worry,' he said again.

Whisky in his tea had ignited his moustache and made his face a merry conflagration.

'When I say it will snow . .'

'He made my Madge tiddley on pudding sauce.'

'. . it will snow!'

'I wouldn't believe a word he says,' said Aunt Alice, 'when he's in drink.'

'In drink? I only had a toothful!'

'Then it's high time we were going.'

Uncle Wallace winked fit to crack a walnut.

'I won't forget,' he promised.

Now there was a lot to do, and in the shortest space of time. I bought and sent off my presents to my parents and to Laylie, posted all my cards and broke up from school in the third week of December. From then on I worked solidly in the shop, needing two pairs of hands and still almost going under in the frantic seasonal shopping spree until, at the stroke of noon on Christmas Eve, Uncle Wallace shot the bolts, put the 'Closed for Xmas' sign in the window and cashed up the overflowing till.

We were due to leave at twelve-thirty but Uncle Teddie's wife arrived purposely a little early.

Under her cloche hat, blue as a lupin in the morning cold, 'Do you mind if I use your telephone?' she said.

Of all my aunts she was the least engaging, so unforthcoming and lacking personality she was always referred to as Uncle Teddie's wife and never Daisy May, her rightful name. Coupled with the vaguely removed and saintly expression of the chronic tinnitus sufferer she had such a peculiar shape and ungainly walk she only looked anything like presentable in the Hall of Mirrors at the fair.

We heard her talking on the telephone.

'Hello.. is that you? Well I just want you to know what an absolute pain in the neck you are. You've got a face like a ruptured duck and you're the biggest old gasbag and scandalmonger for twenty miles around. I hope you have a rotten Christmas, and as for a Happy New Year, I wish you the 'flu, chilblains like hot conkers, and.. and boils all over your big fat backside!'

We were flabbergasted.

'So there!!'

Uncle Teddie's wife, so retiring you never saw her coming till she'd almost been and gone? It couldn't be!

'Who was that?' we clamoured, when we heard the telephone slam down.

'That old frump Mrs Gwenny.'

'Your next-door neighbour?' said Aunt Jessie in amazement. 'She hasn't even got a telephone!'

'I know. But that's what I'd like to tell her if she had!' said Uncle Teddie's wife.

Uncle Wallace was just warming up the engine of his delivery van when Uncle Billy came galloping along the lane holding on to his hat and waving his post-horn.

'Any room for a littl'un?'

'Hop in!'

He did, and in a brace of shakes we were off.

It being only a matter of a few miles or so along white-mantled country lanes from Uncle Reuben's we were there before one o'clock, though still the last to arrive.

In a tinsel sparkle of hoar-frost, excited chatter and rosy cheeks, the farmyard was already full of relatives, stamping feet and huffing foggily into gloves as they waited to get aboard a roomy old boat of a hay-wagon fitted with bench seats and a high handrail. The excitement was catching. Their well-buffed harness elaborate as any

137

medieval trappings, the two pairs of draw horses, Tip and Tap, Luke and Cinders, were fettled up and dancing their hooves in their eagerness to get going.

Bags, bundles and Christmas parcels were soon loaded, including a large wooden box of Uncle Wallace's. Then the ladies were helped up the rear step and made comfortable with travelling rugs and blankets round their legs.

With everybody in their places and Uncle Billy stood up to give a fanfare on his post-horn, Uncle Reuben flourished his whip.

'Hup there, Tip. Hup there, Luke, and off we go!'

The wagon pulled away with such unexpectedness there was instant chaos.

Perched on a tin trunk with no hand-hold, stout little Aunt Tilly somersaulted backwards, nifty as a clown through a hoop, and showed a flaming sunset of red-flannel drawers.

At the same time, with a despairing arpeggio on the post-horn, churchwarden Uncle Billy had been pitched neck and crop over the tail-gate and was sprawling face down in the yard.

'Bugger!' he said when his hat fell off.

'Bugger and damn!' he swore as the wagon backed up and a wheel rim went over the crown of it. 'There goes a hard-earned guinea, and good words into the bargain.'

'Well,' said Uncle Wallace, 'it might have been worse.'

'I'd like to know how.'

'Your head could have been in it!'

Making light of such minor mishaps we started off again with a back-handed crack of the whip which unfortunately lopped in two the stylish ostrich plume of Aunt Millie's Christmas creation. Bleak from the bad language, her ruined feather and poor Aunt Tilly embarrassing everybody with her bright red bloomers – bristling in a fur tippet that looked as though it had just jumped on her out of a tree – Aunt Millie sat bolt upright in her seat and somehow managed a diverting remark.

'Ahem, er – tell me, Wallace, what would you like for Christmas?'

'Beer, bedsocks and a bucket,' he replied.

Aunt Millie looked daggers and icicles.

The frost-bound fields around were midsummer by comparison.

'Only a little joke, Millie,' said Uncle Wallace jovially. 'Why are you glaring so?'

'A woman's frowning glory is her glare,' she answered tartly.

She was clever at things like that. But for some inner quirk of disposition, with her incisive wit and acid turn of phrase she could have been a very funny woman.

In the frosty afternoon her abundant hair had gathered round her forehead in a lovely fine grey cloud.

What a pity her face was always overcast.

That was more than could be said for the sky.

Although the wind was cold enough there didn't seem to be a snowcloud in sight. Climbing steadily upwards with Shaley Clee in the background we passed the time singing a medley of carols but half-way through 'O come all ye faithful', growing more fidgety as we progressed, I clambered up to sit beside Uncle Reuben in the driver's seat.

'It's going to snow,' he reassured me. 'I'll bet you a bob. Now just sit back and enjoy the ride.'

When we turned off the metalled road shortly afterwards I saw the wisdom of using the horse-drawn wagon. Not only could it transport a good many passengers in one go, thereby adding conviviality to the occasion, it was also the only conveyance capable of negotiating the ever-steepening unmade track up to Miss Addie's which to cars was wellnigh inaccessible.

The wind grew chillier yet.

'The north wind do blow,' quoted Uncle Reuben, turning up his collar.

Five minutes went by. Then ten.

'And we shall have snow,' he said, coaxing his team round a twisting bend onto the more exposed slope of Pitchley Edge.

Hidden from view until then, to my delight the northerly sky was packing up with clouds like flocks from a riven mattress and at that moment, as delivered on time as one of Uncle Wallace's carriage-trade orders, it began to snow.

'Where's my bob then?' smirked Uncle Reuben.

'It's worth that and more,' I said, 'not to have a green Christmas.'

'No fear of that up here,' said Uncle Reuben. 'They've been white every year save two since eighteen-eighty.'

'Who told you?'

'Only Jones, and he should know.'

Not to anybody in particular, 'I've been wanting to put that old frump in her place for ages,' I heard Uncle Teddie's wife say. 'I feel better now.'

'I should have brought my Madge,' said Aunt Alice, 'but the children would have chased her and pulled her little tail.'

Momentarily people seemed occupied with their own thoughts, so I retreated into mine.

Sitting just that bit apart, still erect and conversing neither right nor left, Aunt Millie looked on and beyond a rapidly whitening landscape with a smile on her blenched as a cut dipped in vinegar.

Christmas Eve, eight o'clock and all well, turning fine and clear after the wind had abated and the snowstorm blown itself out for the time being; left were only the immutable high heavens, a firmament of ravishing sapphire-blue, and myriad points of light in endless celestial starfields, so far away I knew, and yet so near at hand I might have gone out into the knee-deep snowbound yard and effortlessly plucked them down as Christmas lanterns or decorations for the tree.

Brought earlier in the day in a wagon of their own, itself a special treat, nine or ten assorted cousins had long since hung up their stockings and been whisked off to their dormitory under the farmhouse eaves by Uncle Teddie, who loved children, stealthily followed by Uncle Wiley – who didn't – always pleased to settle the unruly with a horrific bedtime story.

The very threat of ghost or bogle was enough to stiffen the sheets to shrouds. Shaley Clee wasn't all that distant, and everybody knew they were down there, down a three-hundred-foot ladder of bad boys' bones and tow-rope, Clipfoot Jack and Scraggie Aggie in their red-eyed cave, choosing with care their noisome fare, soot soup, tomtits-on-toast, devilled crow and truffles of rats.

If a Christmas goose had been hard to come by, roast naughty boy or girl with all the trimmings would be just as good to munch on, washed down with nips of nightshade gin and turpentine.

Thus thanks to Uncle Wiley the house was invested with surpassing peace, as befitted the holy eve of Christmas. Time enough for it to be given over to din and dinner on the morrow.

Somewhere in the domestic outer reaches of the rambling farmhouse, attended to by a full array of bustling aunts in aprons, everything was being prepared for the coming feast; the poultry plumped up to the parson's nose with two kinds of stuffing, the bread sauce fragrant with cloves, the bacon rolls and every manner of garnishment,

141

not forgetting a choice of plum and figgy puddings laced with thre'penny joeys like silver grapeshot and stacked in cannonball order as if to mount a siege.

And to crown the centre of the table, a pig's head like a bandmaster.

Boots undone and enjoying a quiet drink of pokered ale under the flitch-hooks, hung now with holly and ivy, rosemary, sweet bay and mistletoe, my uncles were lounging about the roaring log fire, spinning yarns, telling the tale, cracking cobs and filberts with their teeth and chuckling at all the old raked-over chestnuts once again in season.

Whereas my aunts soon mustered up places for themselves in the numerous accommodations and hidey-holes of the household, the menfolk had elected to bunk on the hayracks in the brick-built barn across the yard and Uncle Wallace invited me to join them.

I was overjoyed.

In just one bound I had cleared the fencing dormitory for ever and had manhood conferred upon me. The dog in the wheel of the turning year, this was my accolade, my acceptance and admittance at a stroke. I would never look back now.

I must have grown an inch in stature where I stood.

'A natural progression,' said Uncle Wallace mildly. 'When boys have been boys, it's time men were men.'

Towards ten o'clock, with the wind getting up again and more snow in the offing, we said goodnight and headed for our quarters in the barn.

Holding a storm-lamp aloft, in a soft cocoon of star-bright light I led the way across the drifted snow-plains of the yard.

'Br-rr, it's warmer than this in Siberia,' said someone behind me.

'How do you know? You've never been farther than Colwyn Bay!'

'Feel my nose. It's cold as a witch's tit!'

Uncle Reuben and Uncle Wallace brought up the rear lugging the iron-banded box the latter had not let out of his sight all day.

Once they got a farrier's brazier going in the middle of the floor and lit a couple of lanterns, the thick-walled barn could well ward off a weather probing every nook and cranny, made just as snug as the farm parlour, which, when we left, the finished aunts had taken over for a glass of rhubarb wine and a fireside chat while they took the chill off their nighties.

During the journey to the farmhouse I thought a lot about my family and Laylie, but having arrived I experienced a curious sense of detachment from the outside world. As I stretched my legs in front of the brazier it came over me again. The day had been a tiring one, but here I was, and here was where I wanted to be; with my gusty band of uncles, a country Christmas – complete with counterpane of sent-to-order snow – surrounding me, God in His Heaven and the world all right, His peace and goodwill, His lasting joy and gladness, come down on every side.

Counting my blessings, the oft-told story of Christmas cattle-stall and cowshed came to mind, but long before I could see for myself whether it was true the animals of field and fold did kneel at midnight in facing reverence to that lowly crib in Bethlehem, alas, I fell asleep, determined to stay awake.

Tah-tah tah-tah, tah-tah tah tah-tah tah . .

Wafted away who-knows-where by the new-mown scents of summer, wild thyme, clover and sun-dried meadow flowers, first thing Christmas morning, after a night in which it had snowed again with a vengeance, I was roused from the sweetest of hay-borne slumbers by

143

the sound of redoubtable Uncle Billy, up to his flap-pockets in the yard – stood on a brick he was only five foot two – playing 'Christians awake, salute the happy morn' on the post-horn.

All around me, collapsed in the hay as though they had been flung from a parapet, uncles began to stir from attitudes of deep repose.

A brown-coloured greatcoat shuddered and groaned beside me . .

'Tell him where to put that trumpet, somebody!'

. . though another was more tolerant.

'Oh, let him be. He looks forward to it. He tied a knot in his handkerchief last night so's he wouldn't forget.'

'I'd like to tie a knot in his neck!'

'And a merry Christmas to you too!'

Another coat was heaving up.

'Well it wouldn't fit, would it?'

'What?'

'The trumpet.'

'I could give it a start,' offered the first, in a threatening hump.

After I went to sleep they had opened the wooden box and begun in earnest on its contents, Uncle Wallace's pumpkin rum. Of one accord not to expire in the night of frostbite, they emptied two quart bottles between them, knocking it back by the jorum where only a modest glass could clout a temperate man insensible.

Uncle Reuben was the worst affected, with Uncle Wallace close behind.

'Oh dear,' he said, fumbling all about him.

His morning-after eyes hung down like loose buttons on an overcoat.

'Has anybody seen my head?'

Snorting and wheezing, coughing and sneezing, in dishevelled ones and twos they stumbled from the nocturnal fug of the barn into a very Jack of a frost that nipped their fingers, chapped their cheeks and froze their toes to radishes. Floundering across to the farm scullery they boiled a kettle, had a wash and shave, and then – bits of lint or paper stemming the slips to chin and chawl – gargled their way through pints of tea out of the gallon harvest teapot till they were better braced to face the morning.

In the meantime, proposing to serve the dinner as the clock went one, dedicated aunts were already up and about, putting a regular flock of turkeys into the ovens and tackling the hundred-and-one other tasks relating. Pride was at stake, and timing to a 't'. They would never hear the last of it, or so they thought, if a bird had stood too long or the gravy had a skin on it.

As to the men, the long-established walking of the parish on Christmas morning was out of the question owing to the depth of snow. They all agreed on that. And not without relief. Two of Miss Addie's farmhands had dug and swept a path to get about by, so a brisk trip round the courtyard was voted next best thing.

On my second lap I met Aunt Millie, well wrapped up, come out to get a breath of air.

'Good morning, Aunt Millie,' I greeted her. 'The compliments of the season. I like your Christmas hat.'

At once I knew the folly of a hand that's played too far.

In the clearest bell-like tones,

'Mr Grover Wheelkins,' she said.

'Wh-what?' I stammered.

'Mr Grover Wheelkins, the soppy curate in *Love is Only Vanity*,' said Aunt Millie, with that blenching smile again. 'I've read the book as well, my lad, and scotched your little game.'

I swallowed hard.

'You mean you knew?'

'Yes!'

'All the time, you knew?'

'Yes!'

'Then why did you let me go on like that, making an out-and-out fool of myself? Why?' I demanded hotly.

'Because I'm like that,' said Aunt Millie.

Wanting nothing more to do with her, let alone have her spoil my Christmas, I turned abruptly on my heel and left her to her triumph in the bitter frosty yard.

Sitting by myself on the flitchpew in the parlour – happily Father Christmas had had the foresight to deliver the children's stockings upstairs – the prospect of opening presents of my own soon relieved my troubled brow; and when a culinary zephyr of good cheer, the smell of Christmas dinner, started to pervade the downstairs rooms I forgot about Aunt Millie altogether.

Louisa the parlour-maid came in to make up the fire and then Miss Addie to sit and talk to me for a while. She was now ninety-one years old, hale and hearty still, and independent enough to get about unaided except for an ebony stick. Sometimes she had a twinge of rheumatics, but would be better, she decided, when the sun shone on both sides of the hedges.

Attracted too by the delicious aroma of the cooking, fresh from making a snowman in the yard, some uncles began to edge into the parlour, warming their other faces at the hearth, and waiting.

Counting Miss Addie's servants – who always ate with the family at Christmastime – over thirty adults and children would be sitting down to dine, and towards noon any husbands handy were pressed into service by a detail of aunts come in to set the table. Laid up and decorated, with red chenille undercloth and white overlay, fruit and nuts for centrepieces and a gold-and-silver cracker at every right hand the long farm table looked a work of art and would just seat everybody in a good-tempered sort of jostle.

146

Timed to perfection as the grandfather clock in the stairwell proclaimed the hour we took our places, Miss Addie at the head of the table, and in from the kitchen came the uncles with the heavy dishes – the fine pig's head, four prize turkeys and a great fat goose – then in their wake a retinue of aunts carrying platters of vegetables and sauce-boats swimming to the brim.

What a carving and cutting of white breast-slices and juicy brown meat there was, and what a shouting-out for legs and wings and titbits; what a dishing-up and piling-on of accompaniments, of sage-and-onion and chestnut stuffing, little sausages and fluffy bread sauce, roast potatoes, firm green sprouts and parsnips, all poured round with lashings of rich brown gravy.

And what a setting-to there followed, once the plates were filled and passed. Loud as swordplay, the sound of clashing cutlery was battle at its height, subsiding only when, the first plate downed and dealt with, people came back for second helpings, and some of them – Uncle Billy for one – a record third.

In the end his belly got so big and round Uncle Teddie said it looked like he was wearing his bum at the front.

'For shame, our Teddie,' said Uncle Billy, colouring up. 'What a thing to tell a man!'

Not that he much outshone the other uncles.

Doing themselves proud, the more they tucked in the more they blew out, puffing like grampuses, easing collars, loosening belts and letting their tummies rumble, till at last, waistcoat buttons firing broadsides and braces creaking like ship's rigging in the wind, even they were stuffed to the gills and satisfied.

Alone in a welter of discarded drumsticks and skeleton ribs as bare as xylophones the bandmaster-pig surveyed the rout, so aghast at the catastrophe – where once had been a bounty – the lemon had dropped from his stricken jaw and one of his ears was drooping.

147

After the pudding, port and nuts concluding, came the uncles' toast and general verdict.

It was, they said, the best Christmas dinner they had eaten all year; yes, even better than last year's: but not, they hoped, with wives the like of theirs, as good as ones in years to come.

And so said all of us.

Christmas high tea was deferred to Boxing Day when everybody would feel more of a sweet tooth, but after a long and comfortable snooze by the fire until it was dark again outside, a substantial supper was put out – legs of ham and pork and the good old country standbys, flash-in-the-pan, Jennie Jones and snap-apple pie.

With the joints went hot diddle dumplings or thick slices of leg-o'-me-drawers pudding served steaming in the cloth.

Supper over, the rest of the evening was the time for entertainment.

Gathered round the fire in one harmonious family which fanned out to the extremities of the parlour, everybody who could, or would, had to do something – play the piano, contribute a song, give a recitation – show willing somehow, even if it was only to ask a riddle or perform a conjuring trick we'd all seen countless times before.

And so they mimed and did impressions, balanced plates, sang ditties and joined in the chorus, and told jokes and laughed themselves silly between-times.

As the evening lengthened, coming into his own in a lowering of the lamps and flickering flames and shadows, Uncle Wiley told such a frightening ghost story it gave us forty fits. Scalps crawled and caught breath fluttered in the gullet more trapped than netted thrushes. So much so that when somebody came up behind Uncle Wallace and inadvertently touched him on the shoulder his mince pie spun out of his hand like a yo-yo and his tongue fell out like a velvet strap.

It was the moment to repair the nervous system with a nightcap.

So lovingly bottled off in mid-December by Uncle Wallace, and protected from accident by joiner's shavings in the wooden box, Uncle Reuben fetched a couple of bottles apiece of pumpkin rum for the men and pumpkin brandy for the ladies.

It was also a moment I had been awaiting with some interest.

Having refused the leg-o'-me-drawers pudding on principle – with an unforgiving glance at Aunt Tilly for her misdemeanour in the wagon coming up – after an assurance as to its cordial and restorative qualities Aunt Millie condescended to accept a little pumpkin brandy.

She drank a glass, and tried another.

Then,

'Did I ever tell you about Wilbur, the trumping pig?' said Uncle Teddie.

He had a roughish sense of humour, never knew where to draw the line and had once shown me something extremely rude with a Captain Webb matchbox. Considering him vulgar, Aunt Millie looked away and pretended not to listen. At certain times her nose grew so long and pointed she might have been tweaked out of the water and saved from drowning by it.

It was also getting very rosy.

'Well,' began Uncle Teddie, when they all replied no, not that they could remember.

It wasn't much of a story as stories go; only that Uncle Teddie had once had a pig called Wilbur and by chance one day a block of kitchen soap had been ground up with the pigswill. The pig had snuffled up a whole trough of it, which resulted in a monumental flatulence.

That was all really.

Apart from 'He swelled up so much,' said Uncle Teddie, 'I swear, I had to peg him down with a string in case he lifted off and flew, and every time he trumped he sailed up like a balloon and filled the sty with handsome coloured bubbles. Such a look of wonderment as came over that pig's face I never saw, and never shall again.'

He ended on a level tone, and there was no reaction for a minute. The yule log made a shower of sparks and settled in the grate, Uncle Teddie tamped his pipe and struck a match, and one or two uncles murmured well fancy that, and would you credit it?

And then – unheard before in living memory – an unearthly sound, beginning small, came strangely to our ears. Trying to contain itself, it couldn't; trying to hold in, for propriety's sake, it failed; shaking loose, vibrating the floor, rattling the walnuts in their bowl and causing dust-devils in the fireplace, it tore up the walls and ran amok along the ceiling, threshing the holly and mistletoe like besom brooms and searching frantically for means of exit.

Blended by devious alchemies into a cozening draught or elixir, two glasses of pumpkin brandy – plus the mental picture of Wilbur the flatulent pig, lost in wonder and washday bubbles – had got Aunt Millie . . laughing.

She tittered, she giggled, she rocked back and forth, and finally, all dignity gone to kingdom come, threw back her head and let herself go in peals and gales and fits and stitches.

Such a look of wonderment as came over everybody's faces I never saw.

And never shall again.

'Oh . . oh,' cried Aunt Millie. 'I never laughed so much in all my life. I don't give a tuppenny damn for anybody.'

She got up and whirled around in a carefree jig.

150

'And I want to go out. Out, I tell you! I want to go out into the big wide world . . and . . and throw a snowball at the moon!'

Long after they had persuaded her to go to bed instead, about three in the morning, fast asleep in the barn I was awakened not by the sound of laughter but that of copious weeping. None of my uncles, embedded in the hay again, seemed to have heard it, so climbing over the litter of bodies to investigate I peeped through a crack in the barn door and out into the moonlit yard.

Clad only in her long cotton nightgown Aunt Millie was standing in front of the snowman the uncles had made on Christmas morning.

And crying inconsolably.

'Oh-h, snowman . . snowman,' she sobbed, 'what have I done? What am I going to do? I'll never be able to look them in the eye again.'

Dressed in a raggedy scarf and Uncle Billy's church-warden hat, the snowman withheld advice or any comment.

'Oh yes, I know. You can't reply,' went on Aunt Millie. 'You're frozen-hearted, same as me. But I had to talk to somebody.'

She was wringing her hands now in despair.

'I don't know why I'm like I am . . stuck-up, stand-offish, all the things they say about me. I'm a wasp and I know it. Got to sting and hurt, no matter what.'

Coming closer Aunt Millie straightened the snow-man's hat and tidied his scarf across his coal-buttoned chest, something I had never seen her do for Uncle Dick.

'Two for a pair, me and you, old snowman,' she confided. 'Like you can't speak, I can't explain my feelings. And I can't give. I can't! I haven't got it in me, to bend a bit, and give. Sometimes I'd give the earth to make it up . . but for all I can do, I might as well take a snowball and . .'

151

She broke off as she became aware of me out of the corner of her eye, standing there in my pyjamas and slippers.

'What's the matter with you, boy?' she said, angling her head all sharp and haughty.

'Nothing, Aunt Millie.'

'Have you been spying on me?'

'No, Aunt Millie.'

'What then?'

'I heard a noise. It woke me up.'

Attempting to retrieve some of her self-respect, pulling it about her like an imaginary shawl, 'I . . I just came out to throw a snowball,' said Aunt Millie. 'Nothing more.'

'How about if we throw one together?' I suggested. 'Then we can both go back to bed.'

Solemnly we made a snowball each and took aim over the roof of the barn at a moon now moving behind it on its nightly homeward run.

I went first.

'Not bad,' said Aunt Millie, throwing hers.

I was surprised how hard it went, propelled with much more strength of purpose, at the target.

'Not bad yourself, Aunt Millie,' I told her.

Then I said

'Come along now, Aunt Millie. You'll catch your death out here.'

Seeing her to her room and into bed I tucked the bedclothes in and covered her with the eiderdown.

'There,' I said, 'you'll be as right as ninepence in the morning.'

Aunt Millie reached out to touch me.

'You're a good boy,' she said, 'and I love you. It's . . it's just that I . . I can't seem to . .'

'I know,' I said gently. 'Goodnight, Aunt Millie.'

'No, wait,' she said.

152

More than said; a voice inside a voice implored me from the depths of her.

'You're going on to be a man now,' said Aunt Millie, 'and there's not much I can tell you, except . . if you're ever up against it, and that wound up inside it's like you're going to burst . . well, you think on your old Aunt Millie, and go out . . and throw a snowball at the moon.'

'We missed though, didn't we?' I said.

'It's not that, boy,' replied Aunt Millie, and I clearly heard the voice within a voice again. 'When try as you will you can't evade the issue, nor fight against your lot . . it's not the useless gesture, it's just the show of damn' defiance to the last!'

I knew nothing of what it was that plagued her, only that suddenly I felt closer to her than I ever had before. Doing something I never thought I would – giving her a kiss – I went towards the bedroom door.

'I'm sorry if I spoiled your Christmas,' said Aunt Millie.

Very far from that, she made it.

★   ★   ★

153

★ **12** ★

★

I didn't know why I found myself telling Aunt Belle about the Great Tone.

That and Uncle Lloydwillie.

Sitting by ourselves in the farm parlour the day after Boxing Day – she had asked me to come and see her when I had a moment – it just came out in the conversation.

But it was conversation I was having to make, talking for talking's sake. On pins and needles in my chair I had a premonition, if not exactly now, in the near future all might not be well with me.

'It was on top of Bob Major Clee,' I began. 'We'd had a picnic and we were talking about music. All of a sudden Uncle Lloydwillie took my hand and said "Music? If you've got anything about you, you've only to tune in, and there it is." And then I heard it.'

'Heard what?' said Aunt Belle.

'The Great Tone Uncle Lloydwillie called it,' I told her, going on to quote him word for word. 'The song of all the earth, the unison of nature . . pitched on a constant D, lower than the lowest organ note, higher than the highest violins can reach . . made by the four winds and seven rolling seas, the resonating mountain peaks, the sound of waterfalls and rivers . . the voices of trees, the choirs of the forests . .'

'Mad,' breathed Aunt Belle, quite caught up and captivated.

'. . the height and depth of all that Is, the never-failing hallelujah God hears, standing on His Doorstep.'

'Mad as a sharrabang of loonies!'

'Who, me?'

'No,' she said firmly. 'Him!'

'The funny thing is,' I went on, 'the minute Uncle Lloydwillie let go my hand I couldn't hear a thing. Now how do you explain that?'

'He baffles explanation, that man,' replied Aunt Belle.

'I asked him how he did it . .' I said.

'I gave up trying years ago.'

'. . but all he would say was "Electric boots!" '

'And did he give that infuriating grin of his?'

'Yes.'

'Tck, him and his Welsh Wall!'

'Then "Me and Beethoven", he said. "Both with electric boots and both at one with nature." '

Aunt Belle's sigh was long and unduly heavy.

'Never the same since he spent the night alone on Cader Idris.'

'You mean that time he went in search of the Chair of Idris?' I said. 'To sit in it?'

'He was half daft when he went up there, but poet or madman, whatever it made him, I put him beyond all bar the final reckoning now.'

Uncle Lloydwillie dismissed as past redemption, at any rate in this life, there the conversation ended. Although I had rambled on enough; it was up to Aunt Belle to provide a change of subject. Welsh-houseproud – keeping up with the Joneses that meant! – careful to roll the mat up when she went out in case of sparks, favouring necklaces of jet and with a mercury glass witch-ball hung up in the window of her little terrace house, she was a genuine sensitive and clairvoyante.

Loving wife of Uncle Joss the steeplejack, darkly cast and thrifty – she, if anyone, could make a shilling do the work of two – people came from miles around to see her.

With me it was a now and then occurrence, that sensing of a parallel dimension once removed from ours. It came close when I ignored it, and, to my impatience with myself for striving, took flight when I tried too hard to enter. With Aunt Belle it was different. Aurally serene she passed in and out at will, the light along her way ever a steady radiance, while for me it was merely – and only – the sometimes flashes in the egg of fog.

Presently there looked to be no sign of the talk continuing, unless I made an effort to revive it.

'Er –, you did ask me to come and see you, Aunt Belle,' I reminded her.

Silence in the parlour had caused me to count the green silk tassels on the antimacassar several times over.

Being thirteen, they did nothing to improve the promptings of my imagination.

'Can it be true, I wonder . .' she said at length.

Something she would have to tell me had arranged her features impassively.

'. . that note of nature's, that hallelujah, and God stood listening on the doorstep?'

But it would be in her own time.

'Uncle Lloydwillie says it is.'

She would not be hurried.

'And why is it a D?'

'Who knows?' I said. 'Pachelbel's canon is in tune with it though. And that's why Handel wrote the Hallelujah Chorus in D major. To fit in with the everlasting praise and glory.'

'I suppose that's another bit of the gospel according to Lloydwillie?' sniffed Aunt Belle. 'There's no catching him napping, I'll give him that!'

'He says if ever the Great Tone should cease . .'

'Do tell me!'

'. . the earth would be rent asunder, and all the windowpanes of Heaven crack and shatter as from a multitude of housebricks.'

There was a pause.

Aunt Belle picked remotely at a fingernail.

All at once she seemed to have had enough of Uncle Lloydwillie.

Or my obvious hero-worship.

'I hope it isn't on a Thursday,' she said. 'I do my shopping on a Thursday.'

'Is there something you want to tell me, Aunt Belle?' I asked her.

Just then I couldn't be certain which were blacker – or more dispassionate – the string of jet beads across the salt-cellars of her throat, or her unnervingly penetrating eyes.

'I wouldn't look forward to the New Year,' she said. 'Not if I were you.'

★　　★　　★

★ 13 ★

★

Slipping and sliding, skidding from one side of the snowbound track to the other and holding on to the handrail for dear life, we came down from the farmhouse on the last day of December. Uncle Reuben knew a thing or two about horses and how to handle a full wagon-load in conditions as daunting as a bobsleigh run. If there were thrills, there would be no spills; we were safe in his skilful hands. Using the old-time carters' trick of bookend-rig – a pair of horses fore and aft, one to lead and the pair at the rear about-faced to dig in and control the descent, he brought us down in style to the level road where he could re-hitch the team and proceed in normal fashion.

Even so the horses' hooves had to be tied with sacking.

Arrived at his own farm we took our leave of all the aunts and uncles and soon Uncle Wallace, Aunt Jessie and I were in the van and heading for village, shop and a welcome home from Auntie Fan and Billingsgate.

We were reduced to three because Uncle Teddie's wife was driving back with Uncle Teddie and the children – who insisted on returning in a party, the way they came – and Uncle Billy had decided to stay on at the farm a few days more, he and Louisa the pretty parlour-maid having, as it were, an understanding. They walked out weekly Wednesday afternoons and fortnightly Saturdays, held hands in church on Sundays and had been doing much the same for the past fourteen years. It was a long time by any standards, so what the understanding was nobody quite understood.

January, for me, was always a month of marking time, the round of seasons noticeably disinclined to stir and be about the business that it should.

Admittedly, October was a standing-still time too, but then at least the air was of relief and resting. The gleaning-sheaf their sign that work was over, deserving men could meet with pipe and pint at the spent field's gate and the ground felt goodly under their feet. Warmed in the setting sun, and hawthorn berries in abound, birds sang no sweeter than when the hedge was decked with rubies.

In January there was no clement air nor satisfaction. Gates were fast with mud and blackened twigs held rarely a joyful bird. The bark of trees burst in the attacking frost and ice groaning and shifting along the banks of Evensong brook could just as well have been another, over-riding, force – the one which knows no rest – grinding its teeth, sharpening its edge tools, at the prospect of a year ahead of toil and turning.

Moving on, albeit very slowly, there came a day two weeks into the new month when, in an afternoon already growing late, my mind was much elsewhere than on the ever-changing, never-changing Land. Looking out of my attic window I was taking in the view without altogether seeing it. Light was scarce, the wick of declining day burned down so low there was barely enough to discern the beginning hills by, and, seeping in at the corners of the window frame, gloaming had fogged the little detail to be had, giving the effect of a poorly taken photograph.

Through the window midwinter's abysmal, dismal want of colour was returning more of a glass-plate negative than a finished picture, and concentration – mulling over words – had further blurred the image.

'Now don't misunderstand me,' said Aunt Belle.

Seeing my face fall she had been quick to reassure me, though the damage had been done.

As disquieting as they were unlooked-for, her brief words of pronouncement had made their mark, casting more than a fleeting shadow over my hopes and expectations for the year to come.

'No deaths or injuries or such,' carried on Aunt Belle. 'Nothing of that sort. Only . . well, I'm told I should prepare you . .'

'Who told you?' I wanted to know at once.

'. . for some . . ups-and-downs in life, that's all. Who told me?' said Aunt Belle. 'Why, those in spirit. The ones who gave their word my man would never die of falling, but in his bed, as any good man should.'

'Hmmph, I wish I was as well looked after,' I commented.

'You are,' said Aunt Belle. 'Believe me.'

'Well what did you mean . .?'

'I mean forewarned is forearmed. So brace yourself for a couple of knocks is what I have to tell you.'

Again my face fell, hearing that.

'When, Aunt Belle?'

'But tackle your problems in good heart. It's all a part of life's unfolding. When?' she said.

Often she seemed to catch up with the question two or three sentences after it was put to her.

'Mm-m, when?' she pondered. 'Sooner than later, I would think. Rather soon than later.'

Back to counting the tassels on the antimacassar, by now I was thoroughly unsettled.

And they were still thirteen, and green.

Looking for means of extrication I had only one line left to follow.

'Who is actually telling you all this, Aunt Belle?' I pressed her. 'How do I know it has to do with me, and that it's going to happen?'

'A lady comes to me now . .'

Aunt Belle folded her hands in her lap and closed her eyes.

'. . I see her holding out . . a matchbox,' she said. 'It's got an insect in it. Yes, that's it . . a spider.'

I was astonished.

Aunt Jessie just might have mentioned the lady in the room – I'd been waiting to ask Aunt Belle about her anyway – but no-one could have known about Lacey.

162

It was impossible.

'You placed him under the floor after he passed on, and said a little prayer.'

Or was it?

As Aunt Belle opened her eyes and narrowed her gaze on me . .

'The lady should be proof to you I do know what I'm saying.'

. . I knew I hadn't a leg to stand on.

Such was my state of caution from that day on, just reaching the end of the month came like a milestone of achievement: the eleven months remaining were the millstone.

Starting my second term at the local school – only a penny bus-ride away – I was a model of correctness getting on and off the bus and looking right and left before I hastened across the road. I also avoided stray black cats and having to walk under ladders and was particularly on the look-out for solitary magpies in the vicinity. One for sorrow was a portent I was better off evading.

Auntie Fan was a real Job's comforter.

When I wanted to borrow the rabbit's foot I knew she kept among the bits of trammel in her handbag she said 'Well, I'll lend it you . . but I don't know though. The rabbit had four, and fat lot of good it did him!'

'Thanks, Auntie Fan,' I said. 'I knew I could rely on you.'

Two a week and sometimes three, Laylie's letters were my only true refreshment. They made me feel like flowers after rain. My head uplifted from my drab surrounds, I read and read them over on the days of their arrival, and whatever might befall, of one thing I was certain: our relationship was built upon a rock.

Not so Uncle Billy's.

'Biblical sand,' he sighed.

163

On the last Saturday of January when he came by as usual with the evening sporting paper from which he and Uncle Wallace checked the football coupons that never won a thing.

'An habitation built upon the sand!'

'What's that then, Billy?' they said.

'Anything to do with women,' he said morosely.

Another reason for his staying on at the farm was that some unkind person had taken his treasured post-horn and hidden it, and he would not go home without it, he declared, not if it meant pulling the place apart – farmhouse, barns and byres – down to the foundations.

He had come away frustrated.

A painstaking search had failed to reveal its whereabouts and only today had he discovered why.

Her conscience sorely troubled and saying she could no longer bear to keep the secret, he had received a letter from Louisa, of all people. Persuaded it was only a prank between brothers, she had been bribed with a ten-shilling note to smuggle the post-horn on to the children's wagon. Uncle Teddie had it at his house and was going to give it back when it suited him, to pay Uncle Billy out for waking him up on Christmas morning.

'Oh, can you imagine,' he said, 'my best intended being party to a thing like that?'

Even Aunt Jessie inviting him to kippers for tea failed to please him.

'It's our Teddie's to blame,' she said, dishing them up. 'He's got no ear for music.'

'And he'd put drawing-pins on the chairs at the Last Supper,' said Uncle Billy. 'We all know that! But no, it's Louisa has fallen badly by the wayside, and I'm seriously thinking of terminating our understanding.'

'Well, Bachelor Billy!'

Aunt Jessie screwed her apron up at the thought of it.

'Don't tell me you'd throw her over, and fourteen years of courting, all for a bit of harmless joking?'

'I would,' he said.

'Then you're a hard man,' said Aunt Jessie.

And took away his kippers.

'Heart of stone,' said little Uncle Billy.

'Unbending and unforgiving,' put in Uncle Wallace.

'Principles of iron,' came the answer.

'If you ask me . .' began Auntie Fan.

'Well I didn't!'

'. . if I was poor Louisa, I'd consider I was well rid.'

'Oh-h, and when I think . .' reflected Uncle Billy.

He wasn't even listening.

'. . the pounds she must have cost me, in teashops and arcades. I was going to send a Valentine, but I wouldn't spend the money now.'

'You mean old skinflint, I'd have you up for breach of promise!'

The next we heard – from the postman on his morning delivery – was that stony-hearted, stern-principled Uncle Billy had been only too glad to kiss and make up, soft as butter, when Louisa paid him a tearful visit to beg his love and forgiveness. They had exchanged Valentines and tokens – a silver snuff-box from her, a carved love-spoon from him – and were thinking of putting up the banns at Easter.

'About time too!' said Aunt Jessie. 'And all's well that ends well.'

'After fourteen years,' grinned Uncle Wallace, 'I should think it's all's well that ends.'

'Good for them,' piped up Auntie Fan brightly. 'An end and a beginning. Spring is in the air, the buds are on the bough. It's time I took some senna pods.'

They laughed aloud, and so did I, to feel the year advancing.

During the previous fortnight all the snow had vanished, even the drifts beneath the hedges, skies had cleared and the sun was staying out much longer. Every morning early a tame old pair of pigeons billed and cooed beside my window, waking me agreeably to milder February days, and by breakfast-time the blackbirds in the garden lilac tree were whistling the back door down.

In coming green and celandines the world was on its way again.

Pleased with life, for once, and with myself receiving not one Valentine but two, I opened them at the table, the first from Laylie, with a nice long letter, the other signed 'Guess who?' – and plainly postmarked Llandafty.

'Oh yes . . and how is Meriel?' said Aunt Jessie drily, opening a letter of her own.

'Crying herself to sleep at night, because I'm such a hit with all the girls,' I smirked. 'Mind you, being so good-looking I can afford to pick and . .'

Glancing across at Aunt Jessie, the playful words died in my throat.

She was ashen.

'Aunt Jessie . . oh, whatever's wrong?'

'It's . . nothing. P'raps you . . you'd just excuse me for a minute,' she managed to say.

When she went through to the back kitchen and quietly closed the door Uncle Wallace picked up the letter which had fallen from her fingers onto the table.

Aunt Fan and I looked at it over his shoulder.

Out of the blue my mother had written to tell us that the house they had moved to being ready much earlier than anticipated, and with my father well established in his new job, they would like me to return as soon as was convenient. They realized it was short notice, and apologized for that . .

'I don't want to go,' I said.

. . but for some time they had also been concerned about my loss of schooling and had arranged for me to make it up, if I could, by commencing next term at a place called St Odred's, a fee-paying private college near where they now lived. So if I could come home fairly quickly . .

'Oh dear,' said Auntie Fan. 'Poor Jessie, how she must be feeling.'

She too went out to the back to see what she could do.

'And I won't go,' I said. 'I want to stay here.'

Shaken by the news himself,

'There is no don't or won't about it,' said Uncle Wallace.

'It's not fair,' I protested.

'Sooner or later it had to come. It's just sooner than the later we expected.'

Aunt Belle's words come home to roost.

In spite of her timely warning, catching me in an unguarded moment in the buoyant mood of spring, the world had ceased its onward course and closed about me like a trap.

'I wouldn't have minded in the summer, when I was supposed to go,' I said. 'I was resigned to that. But Laylie was coming up at Easter, and in the holidays as well. I can't believe it's over. Just when things were going nicely, this has ruined everything and upset all my plans.'

Giving himself time to think, Uncle Wallace poured out two cups of tea, sugared and stirred them slowly, and pushed one over to me.

'Life never does come to us like the picture on the lid of the box,' he said.

'You can say that again,' I muttered.

'We have to work at it. Take the pile of pieces and put them all together the best way that we can.'

'I don't want to go,' I said.

167

'P'raps just here and there we get a glimpse of how it's turning out . . but like it or lump it, it's nearly always too damn' late by then.'

'I want to stay here.'
'It's too damn' late,' he said.

★   ★   ★

⋆ **14** ⋆

⋆

'Got your ticket-money?'

'Yes,' I answered.

'Are you sure?' said Auntie Fan.

I tapped my inside blazer pocket.

'It's in the wallet Laylie sent me for Christmas.'

'And the sandwiches?'

'In my suitcase, Auntie Fan.'

'I made them ham and cheese, the way you like.'

'How about the bottle of pop?'

'That too, Aunt Jessie.'

'And you know where to change stations?'

'Yes.'

'And the times of the connections?' she persisted.

'Like my two-times table,' I told her. 'Don't worry, Aunt Jessie.'

I spoke without thinking, and could have bitten off my tongue.

'Don't worry?'

Her lovely lilting voice was aching.

'I never knew the hour in the day,' she said.

'Well come along then . .'

Uncle Wallace was on edge, I could tell, for Aunt Jessie's sake.

Waiting to go, he stood awkwardly in the kitchen doorway, gripping his bowler hat and telling the brim of it like a rosary.

'. . if you're done with all the fussing. We ought to get a move on.'

'All right,' I said. 'Just let me go and wish my room goodbye.'

It was something I made a practice of wherever I stayed, at friends' homes, with relatives, and especially in those tall bay-windowed rooms in boarding-houses when we holidayed by the sea. There, at Sandy Ridge, in Harbour View or Ocean Villa, I usually left some item of my own – a halfpenny on top of the wardrobe, a button hidden underneath the rug – so I could reclaim it on a subsequent visit.

Possessions always bring you back.

Today it was my 'tater-hawk and Gwilym's tin that I was leaving. They were properties of mine yet, oddly, as unattached as strangers to me now. What earthly use did I have for a home-made bird-scarer, the potato body shrivelled up, the feathers moulting out and falling? And had I really been so immature – or taken in – as to believe that shouting in a tin I could hold the sound imprisoned till I let it free again?

Along with answering the questions it would be difficult to deny that leaving things behind provided an excuse, within the purpose, to discard them as an out-grown part of me, like the moment when I first set eyes on Laylie and I put away my toys.

Placing them on the mantelshelf I caught sight of myself in the mirror above the little blackleaded grate where Aunt Jessie had made me fires to go to sleep by on the coldest winter nights. Face to face with someone – but not the boy I used to be – there came to mind the title of the closing hymn from Sunday evening's service . .

. . 'Now the Day is Over'.

'I know it is,' I said. 'Uncle Billy and Louisa, theirs was an end and a beginning. Mine was a beginning, and now it's at an end.'

In two or three weeks intervening, once the shock of the initial blow had lessened in the house, an air of calm came after the calamity. There was nothing for it but to go and nothing I could do about it, therefore, thinking better of throwing snowballs at the moon, I kept my head and opted for a soldierly withdrawal. The Ready Boys would have retired from an untenable position in proper order, and only lately an entered member of their company I felt I owed them that.

And so I finished at the village school, gradually did the rounds of saying farewell – to aunts and uncles, customers of the shop and all the people I had come to know – and somehow found time for writing every day to Laylie.

The equal of the situation right away, her letters by return were all that I could ask for, a tonic to my outlook and resolve.

Lastly, keeping just a small case to travel with, I had packed my clothes and an accumulation of other belongings into a plywood tea-chest and sent them off by railway van the day before.

Everything attended to, it was time for me to go.

'Well goodbye, little room . .'

How happy I had been there, up among the slates and stars.

'. . and goodbye, lady,' I said.

Where there had been a reservation in accepting me, such warmness was extended now, such evident regretting that I had to leave.

'Thank you for being near and taking care of me. Although you never let me see you, I knew that you were there.'

Startled by a footfall on the stair I looked towards the open door but it was only Aunt Jessie, come to see if I was ready.

'I'll say ta-ta up here,' she said. 'I'm not too good at partings as a rule.'

'Nor am I, Aunt Jessie.'

I wrapped my arms around the big soft motherly spread of her.

'Except for "I'm going to miss you so", there's not much I can say. If all else fails when we get lonely, let's give a thought to good old Only Jones.'

'Whyever him?' she said.

'Don't you remember my fortune in the tea-cup?

''Where you are you will not stay, but come again another day.'' '

Aunt Jessie went to sit down by the window.

'I hope you will,' she said. 'I dearly hope you will.'

'And one more thing,' I said. 'That letter, asking me to come home. They got the wording wrong. I know they're my parents and I wouldn't want to hurt them, but it's like I felt at Christmas. Here I am and here is where I want to be. This *is* home, and anywhere else is somewhere else to me.'

It was a moment or two before I went out of the room but Aunt Jessie neither turned nor spoke to me again.

'And that's how you left her?'

'Yes,' I said. 'She was all right though. I thought Aunt Jessie was ever so brave, considering.'

'She'll do her crying on the inside,' said Uncle Wallace, 'and sit beside that window for a long long time to come.'

'I'm sorry about that, Uncle Wallace.'

'It can't be helped,' he said.

'No, I suppose not.'

'Anyway, it was a nice sentiment, about your home being here and not somewhere else. You didn't have to say it.'

'Oh yes I did.'

'Blessed if I know why!'

'Just look around,' I said, 'and there's your answer.'

My last view of the shop was from across the green, with Auntie Fan stood at the door holding Billingsgate in the crook of her arm and waving his paw at me. Forty minutes later we were high up on Claypot Mount, a well-known local landmark, surrounded by the enchanting beauty Uncle Wallace was too familiar with to make a point of noticing.

173

Because I didn't feel up to another string of goodbyes from Mrs Maudie Garbett in the garden, and Daddy Rhys and Dobbin – also, at Trucklebed Farm, Gwilym would have been sure to ask me about the tin – we were walking to Clanetty station by a different route, via the Pennytown crossroads, then up a long and winding field path skirting the summit of the Mount. From there we could look down on the railway bridge and the thin steel thread of the branch-line running through the cutting.

All around us lay the land.

Hung in balance in blending shades of blue, the timeless hills were shimmering in the upland wind that sang for ever, newborn clouds were little as lambs in the sky and in the early March morning air catkins along the way hung from bare branches like a rainstorm captive on a stick.

A magical, mystic province, ethereal and There, all around us lay The Land.

'Well, I'm looking.'

After the climb Uncle Wallace had been regaining his breath on a cairn of stones on the brow of the hill.

'And very nice it is too.'

'Very nice?' I said. 'It casts a spell over me. I felt it from the start, like being part of it somehow and never wanting to grow up. Though in the mirror this morning I could see I must have, in a way.'

'By leaps and bounds,' said Uncle Wallace, 'compared with that harum-scarum lad of just a while ago. Now it's long trousers, shaving . .'

'Only twice a week,' I said.

'. . all sorts of improvements, and a lovely steady girl as well. And you've had a few adventures . . Uncle Will's money, the squire's wine, and so on. Your Aunt Jessie even got her toilet at long last, and if that isn't progress I don't know what is. So looking back, you can't say life's been dull.'

'It's not looking back that bothers me,' I said. 'Coming, I knew where I was coming to. Going, I don't know where I'm going.'

'On.'

'On where?'

'Just on,' said Uncle Wallace, pushing his bowler hat back on his forehead.

The most uncomplicated of men, seated on the cairn, billowing and imperturbable – pink of flesh and so much larger than life, astride a barrel he could have been the patron saint of breweries, painted by Rubens – it was more than I could do not to rush to him and let him hug me to his ample middle as I had when I arrived last summer.

'Onward and upward . . hail, rain or sunshine, like we have to do.'

'It . . it's hard.'

'Damned hard, sometimes.'

Then,

'Is that a sniffle I hear,' he asked me, 'coming from round about my watch-chain?'

'N-no,' I sniffled.

'Just as well,' he said. 'When boys have been boys, it's time men were men.'

It wasn't the first time he had used the phrase in the last month or two and I wanted to know what he meant by it.

'Nothing, except I know you've proved your manhood. You're not a young lad any longer,' said Uncle Wallace. 'I heard you, creeping in at dawn that cold October morning. The sixth and eleventh stairs up to your room, they creak and give the game away.'

'I'd only been out mushrooming,' I started to excuse myself.

But as Uncle Wallace gave me the look of looks . .

'We've all been out mushrooming,' he said, 'in our time.'

. . the jig was up and I knew it.

'Well thanks for not splitting on me then,' was all I could find to say.

'It's one of my biggest assets in life,' said Uncle Wallace, 'being taken for a gawby. But I'm a sharp one.'

'I'll remember that.'

'Remember everything,' he said, 'and keep your memory green.'

'I'll do that too.'

Not long afterwards, getting into a compartment just as the whistle blew, I let the window down and waved to Uncle Wallace where I left him, sitting on the humpback bridge.

The *Princess Alice* gave a puff of steam and pulled out of the station.

As off it went, on I went.

On? On where? Just on.

Looking back, for a moment I thought I saw standing by his uncle the spit of a boy who once was me, but when I looked again there was no-one there.

As though I never was, had never been, and nothing had ever happened, Time had stood aside to let me by.

And there I was, gone.

★　★　★